"It's a recipe for heartbreak and regret!"

Grant spoke with sudden, violent intensity. "And you honestly believe that a marriage can still be happy even though all the love is only on one side?"

Now Fran was shocked by the raw bitterness in his voice, and her gaze flew to his face.

"It isn't enough, believe me!"

His words seemed to beat into Fran's brain. She suspected they would even weave themselves into her dreams, oppressing her before the moment of waking, enveloping her in a gray blanket of foreboding. Grant hadn't been referring to their marriage, but his bitter statement sprang from his own past experience, and it applied equally well to them.

It wasn't enough for only one to love....

Books by Valerie Marsh

HARLEQUIN PRESENTS
820—DARK OBSESSION

HARLEQUIN ROMANCE
2676—ECHO OF BETRAYAL

These books may be available at your local bookseller.

Don't miss any of our special offers. Write to us at the
following address for information on our newest releases.

Harlequin Reader Service
P.O. Box 52040, Phoenix, AZ   85072-2040
Canadian address: P.O. Box 2800, Postal Station A,
5170 Yonge St., Willowdale, Ont. M2N 6J3

VALERIE MARSH

dark obsession

Harlequin Books

TORONTO • NEW YORK • LONDON
AMSTERDAM • PARIS • SYDNEY • HAMBURG
STOCKHOLM • ATHENS • TOKYO • MILAN

Harlequin Presents first edition September 1985
ISBN 0-373-10820-6

Original hardcover edition published in 1985
by Mills & Boon Limited

CHAPTER ONE

FRAN gazed round the packed room and prayed that someone would open a window before she collapsed. The air was stifling; thick with cigarette and cigar smoke, and shrill with voices from the weaving, jostling mob. From her corner retreat she watched them elbow each other mercilessly out of the way with cries of, 'I'm *so* sorry, darling!' before proceeding, drinks held on high, to shove a grimly determined passage through another group.

God, what was she doing here anyway? She had always hated these sort of parties with their frenzied, false animation. Nobody ever actually *listened* to anyone else. They were always too busy putting on an act, or casting round in case there was someone more important they had missed—whose notice they must attract if there was the remotest possibility that it could take them a step further up the ladder in their career.

But she was in no position to throw stones, Fran admitted, turning her cynicism on herself—she was here for the same reason. Except that she had only come because she was afraid that if she backed out of another of these affairs, Seth would wash his hands of her altogether. He was already finding it hard enough to get work for her without her making his job more difficult by non-co-operation.

'Be there or else,' he had told her flatly, and in spite of their friendship she knew he meant it.

So she had donned her long white boots and borrowed Sacha's new white fur jacket, swearing to preserve it with her life from cigarette burns and spilled Americanos.

The boots were killing her, and she suspected that whatever originally lived inside the fur had turned white and expired from old age. It was moulting frantically. The long hairs stuck to her sweating neck, making it itch, and she couldn't take the coat off now because her black top was plastered with hairs all down the front. She brushed at them irritably, but her efforts only created static electricity in the synthetic fibre, and a fresh lot flew out of the fur and attached themselves with an audible crackle. She sighed and picked up her drink again. Seth had disappeared; prowling round the room for contacts, she supposed. He would be doing it more because he liked her than from any real hope, and dispiritedly she wondered why she didn't go home and save him the trouble. Really home. Not just back to the flat she shared with Sacha, but back to the valley where she had grown up. She could try to get her old job back in the library and live in peaceful obscurity among people who were more concerned over the effect of the weather on the crops than anything else. No one would notice or care that Fran Lucas had failed to make it in the chancy modelling business.

But in five years the library would be changed like everything else, and the reason she couldn't go back was the same reason she had left in the first place. Because of Grant.

Fran knew what had caused the train of thought. That glimpse of the back of a dark head, seen through the arched doorway into the next room. She didn't go in to get a closer look as she would once have done. It had happened too many times before—that sudden lurch in the pit of her stomach, the wild leap of her pulses and the jolt of hope and fear that died when a head was turned to reveal the face of a stranger instead of the one imprinted in her memory.

If ever it was Grant, she thought, she . . .

What would she do? Turn away, probably, as she had done the last time when their eyes had met across the foyer of the theatre. He had recognised her instantly, even though it had been years since he had last seen her, and the encounter in the heart of London was completely unexpected. As it would have been to her if she hadn't idly read the report of the new play and suddenly his name had leapt out at her.

Grant Mercier. It had to be him, though remembering him from the old days she found it difficult to credit. She would never have dreamed that she would one day see his name up in a West End theatre, the author of a highly acclaimed play. She could only think of him as she had known him, with his mired Range Rover and the trio of Jack Russell terriers at his heels.

But perhaps a landowner and farmer turning playwright was no more surprising than the blacksmith's niece with the tangled, silver streaked mane of hair becoming a model. The difference, of course, was that Grant had emerged successfully from his unlikely background and was now famous. In the last four years he had been photographed, interviewed and quoted until he was familiar to everyone. He was a household name, even in Fran's circle, though it was due less to his ability as a writer, she reflected caustically, than because women everywhere raved over him. Even those who had never been to a serious play in their lives would stay up late to watch him in literary discussion programmes on the television. It didn't matter that they understood no more than one word in three of what was being said; they watched because they were hypnotised by the dark good looks and the quality of his beautiful voice.

Seeing him on the screen gave Fran a curious feeling. To her, it was the cultivated, well-groomed writer who was the stranger, while to all those other women, the powerfully muscled man she had so often seen stripped to the waist, sweating and dusty at harvest time, would have been unrecognisable.

But that was an image shared by few. To the rest he was the celebrity he appeared, and who by contrast had ever heard of Fran Lucas? Only a handful, and those unimportant.

Until these last few few weeks Seth had always managed to get her enough work to keep her going, but the brilliant career had never materialised. The vital, vivid looks which turned heads in the street didn't translate on to film. Something was lost, the spark somehow extinguished, and instead of the arresting beauty of her eyes, the camera showed up her less than perfect nose and too wide mouth.

To Seth's continuing exasperation, the one asset she undoubtedly did possess she was reluctant to exploit. He had told her right from the beginning that if she would take her clothes off he could find her as much work as she could handle. Last week she had given in to his impatient insistence and had a new set of photographs taken, and viewing the result she had to admit he was right. Nobody seeing her portfolio now would give a damn that her mouth was too wide, but still she hung back. Nude modelling had a bad image. Most people—men in particular—associated it with the revolting, girlie mag type of thing rather than advertising, and she had enough problems with men already without adding to them.

Sipping her drink as she pondered, she admitted to herself that basically she didn't like the life anyway. She hadn't got the dedication needed to make her accept the hours of discomfort and boredom. The trouble was that at twenty-three she wasn't trained for anything else and there were few enough jobs for those who were.

She shifted uncomfortably, aware of a pain in her

stomach again. She'd been intending to see a doctor about it, but like toothache it disappeared when she actually got as far as picking up the phone to make an appointment. Either that or the bossy receptionist informed her that the doctor was so busy he couldn't see anyone for three days unless it was an emergency.

Clenching her teeth, Fran began to wish she hadn't allowed herself to be fobbed off. This time it was far more severe and it was beginning to make her feel sick. If she didn't get out of this airless room soon she really would collapse.

Glancing round she caught sight of Seth fighting his way towards her through the press, a trendily dressed, red-haired man in tow. Someone to be nice to, Seth's expression warned her, and she took a deep breath. Flash your smile, she told herself—make an impression. It's what you're here for.

She tried to compose her face, and reaching her at last, Seth said heartily, 'Here she is! The hottest little property in the business at the moment!'

The man's sparse hair was combed carefully forward to disguise his advancing baldness, and his straggling beard half hid a small boil with a greenish head. Fran found herself staring at it, nausea rising in her. She couldn't, she simply couldn't, smile and talk and flirt with this revolting man, no matter what it meant in terms of money.

With only part of her attention on what Seth was saying, she vaguely gathered that the job was a promotion for a new range of shampoos. He was extolling the virtues of her curtain of silver blonde hair, but she scarcely heard him as she took in the other man's expression.

She had seen it often enough before; that look which assessed her in a way that had nothing to do with her suitability for the project. She was sick and tired of it, and of all the other men who presumed she was available when they heard she was a model. She didn't know what other kind of job she could do, but suddenly her decision was made.

Seth went into his sales routine, lifting her hair to display it, but without warning the room dipped and whirled round her and she interrupted him to say desperately, 'Seth, I'm sorry but I feel ill! I shall have to get out of here!'

He frowned, exasperated, but she was beyond caring. The pain in her stomach had become violent and the nausea was overwhelming. She felt her face grow clammy, and Seth's frown changed to one of sharp concern.

He grabbed her arm and piloted her towards the other room where the crowd was marginally less, clearing a path with a forceful shoulder, and ordering, 'Make way for the lady! Somebody find her a chair!'

Someone did, and half-fainting, Fran was lowered into it. Seth tried to make her swallow some water, but she pushed it away speechlessly, convulsed with pain and willing herself not to be sick. Her face was burning with heat now, and eyes closed, she felt a hand placed on her forehead.

Curt with authority, a voice said, 'Call an ambulance!' and hearing it through the waves of pain she knew she must be delirious. Then the spasm of agony passed and she opened her eyes for a second before another wave hit her.

But the brief glimpse was enough to confirm what those deep tones had told her disbelieving mind. This time it wasn't imagination or wishful thinking that had given rise to that sense of familiarity. She felt his hand gripping hers and clung to it weakly; heard the well-remembered voice saying quietly, 'Hang on, Fran. I'll get you out of here.'

She nodded to show she understood and he commanded everyone to stand back. From her other side, Seth demanded resentfully, 'Do you know this guy, Fran?'

Trying to escape the advancing unconsciousness, she managed to whisper, 'Yes,' before blackness claimed her.

She remembered little until she was helped, groaning and wincing, to sit up in bed. The nurse arranged her neatly against the pillows and smiled at her with professional sympathy, brightly offering the consolation that at least she knew she would never have to have her appendix out again.

Some time later a vase of red roses appeared on the window sill and the nurse passed Fran the card with the cryptic message, 'You've really torn it now, darling!' There was no signature, but even if Fran hadn't known Seth's writing it wouldn't have been necessary. The first time they changed the dressing over the incision she knew what he meant.

'It will fade,' the nurse told her. 'In a year's time you'll hardly see it.'

So that was one decision taken out of her hands, Fran thought fatalistically. She couldn't change her mind now if she wanted to. Even Seth would have problems in finding an advertiser who didn't object to a bright, fresh, new appendectomy scar.

Sacha came to see her in the evening, causing a flurry of interest as she strolled down the ward, her lean, thoroughbred body held with conscious elegance as though she were still on the catwalk and her black hair in an impeccable chignon.

'I hope you got your coat back safely,' Fran greeted her. 'Though before you wear it I should spray it with a fixative.'

'I wondered why it was so incredibly cheap, darling,' Sacha said gloomily. 'I ought to know by now that my super bargains always turn out to be disasters.'

She disposed herself gracefully on the bedside chair and studied Fran with commiserating interest. 'You do look most frightfully peaky. I thought appendixes rumbled or something first. I was shattered when this unbelievably dishy man appeared and said you'd been borne off amidst all the drama of sirens and flashing blue lights.' She grinned widely. 'It must have been a wow of a party stopper!'

'Involuntary, I assure you,' Fran returned with a wince. She relaxed herself carefully back against the pillows before adding, 'What unbelievably dishy man?'

Sacha met her eyes, her own bright with interest. 'Why, Grant Mercier, darling. You never told me you were acquainted with a famous playwright.'

'Since I haven't spoken to him in nine years it's hardly hot news,' Fran said evenly. 'I can bore you with my fourteen-year-old recollections if you like.'

She kept her eyes lowered as she spoke. Sacha was her closest friend, but not even to Sacha was she prepared to reveal what only the mere mention of Grant's name could still do to her.

Sacha's expression was inquisitive when she eventually looked up. Raising her beautifully plucked eyebrows, she said, 'He seemed frightfully worried for someone who hasn't seen you in nine years, darling. Terribly in control and unflappable and all that, but worried. He's ringing me later so I can tell him how you are. Officially you aren't supposed to have visitors yet, but they said they'd let me in for a minute because I was bringing your toothbrush and things.'

'Well, don't try to make anything of it,' Fran told her wearily. 'He's married and devoted to his wife.'

'Oh,' Sacha said mournfully. 'Though he was bound to

be, of course.' She caught sight of the Sister's purposeful figure approaching, and went on hurriedly, 'It looks as though I'm about to be tossed out. Don't worry about anything stupid like the rent while you're in here, will you sweetie? Just eat up your lovely hospital dinners and get better. I'll see you tomorrow.'

Fran gave her a feeble smile of thanks and Sacha sauntered away, leaving behind a waft of exotic, expensive perfume.

Closing her eyes, Fran thought it clashed abominably with the all-pervading hospital smell. She drifted off into a morphine-induced sleep and was woken by the rattle of the supper drinks trolley. Afterwards she lay awake half the night, though whether from her memories or the discomfort of her operation she didn't know.

Grant. She couldn't remember a time when she hadn't known him. From the earliest years of her childhood he had always been there, linked in her mind with the big, sandstone house where he lived, up on the hill on the opposite side of the valley.

Fran lived with her aunt and uncle in the small house next to the forge. Probably that was where she had first seen him. She had spent hours as a small child watching her uncle shape the red-hot shoes over the anvil, backing away nervously from the heat and evil-smelling clouds of smoke as he pressed them on to the horses' hoofs to check the fit.

Even from that age she could picture Grant, hands thrust into the pockets of his breeches as he leaned against the wall and discussed horses with her uncle. He would have been twenty when she was six and he seemed like a god to her then. She remembered how he used to smile at her when she was led out by her uncle on her first small pony; his friendly amusement at her excitement when she started to go to shows. He bred show hunters, big, beautiful, impressive animals, and she was ready to burst with pride when he noticed her and gave her advice and help with her pony at the ringside. She was completely unselfconscious with him in those days, and it was only when she grew to her teens that she altered, blushing and stammering and becoming unbearably confused if he spoke to her.

She didn't know why he confused her so much, but she found herself beginning to watch out for him. If she saw his Range Rover in the village she would station herself where she could watch without being seen, and the times when she knew he was away from home seemed curiously flat and empty.

He was often missing for weeks at a time, but when she was almost fifteen he stayed home the whole summer. Her tongue-tied self-consciousness had given way now to a breathless excitement when she saw him, and in those initial, sometimes violent awakenings of sexuality, when the other girls tested their fledgeling powers on the boys from the grammar school, she tried out hers on Grant.

She was very tall even then, and almost fully developed, so that she appeared much older than her years. Only the narrow hips and leggy, awkward grace of youth betrayed that her body's maturity was racing ahead of her mind's, and when she looked in the mirror she saw only what she wished Grant to see, her imagination fleshing out curves and imparting fullness to a mouth that later would be sensual.

Popular and sought after by the boys at school, she refused all their invitations, and while her classmates daydreamed of pop stars and film idols, her dreams were all of Grant. At first they were childish and glorious—scenes in which she was thrown from her horse and lay stunned, and Grant carried her back to his house where she came round to find him holding her hand and imploring her in anguished tones not to die.

But as the summer progressed her fantasies changed, veering wildly between innocence and adult eroticism, and during the long, hot days of July, Grant lost his godlike, unobtainable aura. Suddenly he was a man, a flesh and blood being she could actually touch, possessed of a man's thoughts and desires. She looked at him and watched him with different eyes, the broad sweep of his shoulders and powerful thigh muscles causing a clutch of nervous excitement in the pit of her stomach. In bed she plotted ways to make him notice her, and spent restless nights living dreams that made her burn with heat and strange longings, and the fear afterwards that others might somehow be able to read her secret, shameful thoughts.

But no one suspected, and at the start of the summer holidays she began a deliberate pursuit. She knew that Grant took his dogs on to the hill behind the house most evenings, so after tea she took her own dog over the river and up the long climb the other side. Freed from her uniform she wore shorts to display her long, slim legs, and skimpy sleeveless tops, sometimes choosing old ones which had become too small and clung tightly, drawing attention to her breasts, unrestrained as yet by a bra. Her shorts were the length her aunt considered decent, but once away from the road she turned up the cuffs to make them as brief as possible, and satisfied with the result, continued her climb.

It made her legs ache, and she and Muffin were always breathless when they reached the top, but the times she encountered Grant made it all worth while. She would wave and call—everyone did in the country—and it was perfectly natural to turn and go the same way so that they completed the walk together. At the top of the hill they would always sit for a while on the rock-strewn grass while Muffin and the terriers made excited forays into the bracken for rabbits. She dropped down beside him as close as she dared, calculating the chances of their hands or arms brushing, but wise enough to know, in spite of her dreams, that if Grant ever guessed what she was doing, their meetings would cease.

By the middle of August she was sick with love for him. He haunted her nights and was the first thought in her mind each day as she awoke; wherever she went she carried the image of his dark, tanned face, tormenting herself with visions of his thickly lashed eyes looking into hers with the same love and passion that she secretly nursed for him.

Thoughts of him obsessed her to the exclusion of all else; each day was so many hours to be lived through until she saw him again, and when he began to invite her into the house for a Coke on their way down the hill she sometimes thought she might faint with sheer happiness. His mother had re-married and gone to live abroad after his father died, but the housekeeper was always somewhere about, and he was careful never to touch her, even casually.

She realised it was deliberate and was bitterly disappointed until the day she looked up and caught him studying her with a curiously intent gaze. The expression was instantly shuttered, but inside she leapt with elation. The adult part of her recognised physical awareness in his flared nostrils and oddly intense regard. It gave her a sense of power which she hugged inside her, and her hopes and fantasies magnified.

But he never invited her into the house again afterwards. They still met with their dogs in the bracken above the woods, but something was different—he had withdrawn from her. She fretted, yearning for what she couldn't have, and her despair deepened as the holidays drew to a close. Soon it would be back to school and her uniform, and dusk would fall earlier so that she couldn't make the hour-long climb after tea.

Six more days, then five—the precious time sped by faster. With only four more days to go she sat beside him on the grass and watched him under her lashes, trying to imagine what it would be like to be kissed by him; willing him to turn to her, as though by the power of thought she could make him embrace her.

She was so absorbed that when his arm slid round her it seemed for one startled, bemused moment that she had succeeded, but then he ordered quietly, 'Don't move!' and she saw the adder gliding silently from the bracken towards her.

In the same calm voice, he said, 'They're perfectly harmless as long as you don't disturb them. Just keep quite still until it's gone.'

Fran wasn't really frightened. It was adder country and she had frequently encountered them on her walks, though never so close, nor when she was sitting down. But she could not repress a small, nervous shiver as its tongue flicked out and it moved slowly past her leg, watching her with its reptilian eye. It was easily within striking distance, and she felt Grant's arm tighten warningly as he turned his head to follow its progress.

The tension in her changed with that slight movement. Suddenly she was suffocatingly aware of the hard strength of his hold and his fingers pressing into the bare skin above her elbow. Her heart missed a beat, then picked up in pace, and she knew he could feel the heavy thud transmitting through her pulses.

Knew as well, with an insight far beyond her years and experience, that he had not mistaken it for fear. As clearly as though she had told him in words, he had recognised the cause of the sudden clamour within her.

He stiffened, and for a long, unmeasured moment they were still. She was aware of the tautness of the muscles down the inside of his arm and of a faint tremor in his finger, then a thready pulse began to beat insistently in the base of his thumb.

Wild exultation flared in her with the knowledge that he was stirred—that he was reacting as a male to what he could feel in her. When he said finally, 'It's gone,' and the arm round her eased, preparing to pull away, she twisted round with a quick movement so that his hand fell against her breast.

Almost instantly she knew that she had made an irretrievable mistake.

He drew a sudden breath then froze, staring down at his fingers where they rested on the thinly covered swell of flesh. Colour darkened across his cheekbones and he slowly raised his eyes to her face, then snatched the hand away as though it had been burned.

The following day he was gone. Fran lived desolately through the cold and empty winter, and in the spring her aunt told her he was married. She thought her young heart would break from the pain, and lay in bed that night praying that she might die.

CHAPTER TWO

SILENT on her rubber-soled shoes, the nurse said sympathetically, 'Still awake?' and Fran gave her a rueful smile.

'I'm afraid so.'

'You can have another sleeping tablet if you like.'

Anything to keep her from thinking of Grant. She nodded and said, 'Please,' but even after she had swallowed it down, sleep wouldn't come. Pictures and memories flowed back. Not of Grant this time, but of Julia.

Everyone in the village was so pleased he was married at last, though it was eighteen months before he brought his bride home. By then Fran was seventeen and working in the library in the nearby town. Her sense of betrayal was so deep that she had never again crossed the river to the other side of the valley; never went into the forge where she knew she would see an image of Grant leaning against the wall as he always used to.

It was surprisingly easy to avoid him—he was rarely seen in the village now, almost as though the evasion was mutual, but Julia was another matter. She shopped in the village store, visited the elderly, gave prizes in the little school. A lovely woman, Fran's aunt said—she was just the sort of wife everyone would have wished for him, and it was a pleasure to see a couple so much in love and so obviously happy together. She was a Brigadier's daughter too, which was very suitable.

Fran nodded dumbly, and her uncle remarked that she wasn't unlike their young Fran to look at.

'Same colour hair and eyes,' he said. 'And she features her a bit; I noticed it the first time I saw her. They could be sisters, even side by side.'

Aunt Beth allowed it, but said Fran had a long way to go before she could match her in manner.

Oh, Julia Mercier was a paragon, Fran thought bitterly, perfect in everything. They all sang her praises from one end of the village to the other. It was when they began to speculate on how long it would be before there was another Mercier that she knew she had to get away. It was torture enough to run into Grant's wife at every turn, but jealousy would poison her very soul if she had to watch Julia with his children.

When she was eighteen she went with two of her friends to London, but even that wasn't far enough. She could remember with sickening clarity the moment when she had looked across the foyer and seen Grant. It had been five years since that fatal mistake of hers up on the hill, but nothing had changed. Her stomach still seemed to turn over with an actual, physical movement.

He was older, with lines round his eyes which hadn't been there before, but he seemed more handsome than ever—darker somehow in his formal evening clothes, and more lean, though he was still a big man.

Recognition was instant and mutual. Something lit up in his eyes and they stared at one another, then a mask came down over his features and he turned to Julia at his side. Julia, elegant and beautiful, with her serene face and controlled grace, her long blonde hair smoothly coiled on top of her head, her slim figure modestly displayed by her black evening gown.

Watching, Fran saw Grant slip his hand round her waist in a gesture that was lovingly protective. She knew he was about to point her out to Julia. What would he say? Look, darling, there's Fran, the blacksmith's niece from the village?

A wave of jealousy washed over her, so intense it seemed to take her breath, and she whirled away before those beautiful, calm blue eyes could turn to meet hers.

Fran had never seen either of them since. Not until that moment when she had heard his voice and opened her eyes briefly to see him bending over her.

Eventually she slept and woke reluctantly when the day staff came on duty. Annoyingly she was tired all day and she was dozing when Seth came in the afternoon. He asked how she was, then pulled the bench seat up to the side of the bed and sat there, glum and almost silent until she remonstrated with him, asking if he had come to cheer her up.

'Yeah, well.' Restlessly he sat on his hands and rocked backwards and forwards. 'What with one thing and another, it's been that sort of week. And now Libby says she's pregnant.'

'Oh,' Fran said. Uncertain how to react, she settled in the end for, 'I'm sorry.'

'So am I.' His gloom deepened. 'I only wish Libby was as well. She's over the moon. Swears she took her pill every night and she doesn't know how it happened, but I dunno, I've got my doubts.'

'Will you be getting married?'

His eyes rested on her and for a moment he didn't answer, then he shrugged. 'I suppose so.'

Sunk in thought, his gaze strayed to the roses on the sill and Fran said, 'Thank you for the flowers.' She paused, watching him. 'Pay off, Seth?'

'If I couldn't sell you before, darling, I'm not going to be able to do it now you've got a zip up your front.'

'No,' she agreed.

Plainly unhappy, Seth said, 'Face it, darling, you've never been really into it—not how you should be if you're going to get on. We both know there's no glamour in the job itself; it's boring and you're either too hot or too cold. The glamour only comes with the money you can earn if you're at the top, but you're never going to make it. You would have done if you'd stripped off when I told you to, and you perhaps could have cashed in on it now.' He shook his head. 'But as it is, there are too many good-looking birds in competition with you if you haven't got anything to back you up.'

Resignedly, she said, 'I know, and you're right; my heart's never been really in it. I'll look round for something else when I'm out of here. You tried for me, Seth, and I'm grateful, but probably this has happened for the best.'

Relieved by her acceptance he nodded, then said casually, 'Did you ever have anything going with this writer guy who was at the party? Grant Mercier?'

Fran stiffened. 'No. Why do you ask?'

'He came round to the office, looking me over as though I was the opposition. Asked a lot of questions about you as well.' The dark brown eyes regarded her steadily. 'You weren't at your beautiful best before we sent you off in the ambulance so he didn't fall for you then. What gives?'

'I knew him when I was young, that's all. We come from the same village.'

'Which doesn't really explain it,' Seth commented. 'I gave him a progress report, but he could have rung the hospital himself for that. I get the feeling he thinks we're more than just good friends and he doesn't like it.'

'There was never anything like that between us,' Fran denied. Not on his side anyway, she qualified mentally. She pushed back the memory of that brief flaring of light in his eyes when he had first seen her in the theatre.

Seth shrugged, then his eyes went beyond her to the double doors at the end of the ward. Jerking his head to

draw her attention, he said, 'Don't say I didn't warn
you.'

Fran turned swiftly. Grant was talking to the Sister
in her glass office and hadn't seen her yet. She felt panic
rise in her until it seemed to grip her by the throat.
Panic and that other feeling which seemed to drain all
the use from her limbs, and which Grant must never
guess at. She turned back to Seth. He was a good-
looking man in his casual way, and an idea formed.
With desperate urgency, she said, 'Seth, don't leave me
with him!'

He flicked her a quick glance, astute and questioning,
and she felt her face colour as she went on, 'And would
you mind pretending . . . well, what he thinks?'

'You want Libby should kill me?' Seth demanded,
deliberately becoming very Jewish.

'Please,' she whispered. 'There isn't time to explain
now, but please, just this once. He won't come back
again if you do.'

'Okay, darling, I suppose you know what you want.'
Grinning, he added, 'But if Libby ever gets to hear of it, I
warn you here and now that I'll drop you straight in it!'

She smiled her gratitude, and with another quizzical
glance at her, he said, 'Here goes, then,' and leaned over
and kissed her.

There hadn't been time for Fran to wonder how he
intended to carry out her request and her immediate
reaction was shock. His kiss was searching, too intimate
for a public ward, and she was taken aback as she
realised the emotion behind it wasn't feigned.

When he lifted his head she said uneasily, 'Whoa,
boy, you're getting married soon, remember?'

He drawled, 'Final fling,' though his expression was
disturbing. Then it cleared and he stood up, still
holding one of her hands, and she saw Grant watching
them from the foot of the bed.

For a second his dark face held threat and Seth straightened in response to it, and quickly and nervously, Fran said, 'Grant! How lovely to see you! You know Seth, don't you?'

Grant sent him an unreadable glance. 'We've met.'

'I'm surprised we've never run into each other before,' Seth returned easily. 'I don't handle theatrical stuff, but I'm into television commercials and we get round all the premières and showbiz parties pretty well. Does the girls good to be seen at them and get a few free publicity shots with the celebrities.' He looked down at Fran, his smile faintly malicious. 'Perhaps we could set something up with your friend here, darling.' He paused, then added significantly, 'After I've got you home again, of course.'

Fran saw Grant stiffen and cringed inwardly. God, she hadn't meant Seth to go as far as that! But then it didn't really matter what Grant thought of her as long as he never came back to torment and tempt her with something she had glimpsed but daren't put into thought.

Seth had launched into the sales talk she had heard so many times before, exaggerating her trifling successes and painting a golden picture of her future prospects. She couldn't think why until she realised he was linking them together in a way that made it seem they had been lovers a long time. It left a faintly sordid impression. Almost as though he was living off her immoral earnings, Fran thought helplessly, seeing Grant's face grow colder and more tight with every moment.

He looked at Seth contemptuously, then turned his back on him with calculated offence and walked up by the side of the bed.

For a moment he gazed down at her, his mouth rigid, then he demanded harshly, 'Is it true?'

She tried to say yes—it was the whole point of this

charade—but the word wouldn't come. A vivid flush of shame ran up to her hair, and she looked quickly across at Seth who was standing like a graven image, all expression wiped from his face.

Grant took her silence and that quick look for her answer. His jaw tightened. 'I see.'

Meeting his eyes she read an odd mixture there. Contempt? Yes, she would expect to find that, but not the regret or the strange hunger that showed for a split second before he added, 'Good luck, then.'

With a curt nod to Seth he turned away, and Fran leaned back, tears starting to her eyes as her gaze followed his retreating form. When the doors at the end swung shut behind him she took a deep breath, and his tone carefully neutral, Seth enquired, 'Are you sure that was what you really wanted, darling?'

She nodded. 'I thought you went over the top a bit, but it doesn't matter.'

'You mean you didn't want him to think we were having it off?' He shrugged. 'If you're going to do the job at all you might as well do it properly.' He regarded her shrewdly. 'I don't know what's with you two, but you can take it from me he wouldn't be put off by anything else. You didn't see his face when you passed out in front of us. You'd have thought it was his old mother breathing her last at his feet.'

He paused to give her time to weigh his words. 'If you want to change your mind it should be easy enough to find where he hangs out.'

Pain twisted inside her. It wasn't just nostalgic regard that had brought Grant, she knew that as well as Seth did, but his words only deepened the wound. She wondered why she didn't simply tell Seth he was married, but curiously she wanted to protect Grant from any repercussions from his visit and she couldn't trust Seth to remain silent if he knew. Attempting a smile, she said, 'No thanks, Seth, and though I'm sure you're wrong about him, you maligned me with the best of intentions. It's just that we virgins tend to get a bit touchy.'

He stared at her astounded, and exclaimed, 'Oh——! That I *never* thought of! Sorry, darling, but I didn't know they still existed east of Birmingham.'

'It doesn't matter,' she repeated. 'I don't suppose Grant believes they do either, and he's not likely to tell my aunt and uncle back home.'

He continued to stare at her helplessly for a while, then glanced at his watch. 'Hell, I shall have to go! Keep in touch, eh?'

'And you.' She smiled. 'Invite me to the wedding.'

He winced, and still hesitating, reached over to clasp one of her hands. 'Are you sure you don't want me to fetch him back?'

'No.' She shook her head. 'It's a long story, but if I could move any faster than a moderate crawl you'd have seen me start running the moment he came through that door.'

'Women!' Seth said in bewilderment. 'Oh well, take care, darling.'

There wasn't much else anyone could do in hospital, Fran reflected. Each visiting time she watched the doors, tense with that uneasy mixture of hope and dread, but Grant never came again.

When she got home, Sacha fussed over her and friends called, and once Christmas was over she began to apply for jobs. She found she wasn't as lacking in qualifications as she had feared. One thing she did know inside out was make-up and how to apply it, and she got a job in a large department store, demonstrating and selling one of the more up-market brands. The pay wasn't brilliant, but it was steady nine till five-thirty work and she got paid at the end of the week, which was something. The haphazard rewards of modelling had always worried her.

She didn't need to live on a perpetual diet either. She lost the exaggerated slenderness required for the camera and decided she liked herself better with a more rounded figure. The scales would have gathered dust if it hadn't been for Sacha's agonised weight watching. The winter parties were in full swing, and Fran heard her wails of despair as she pored over her calorie chart one day.

'Avocados!' she screamed. 'Fran, have you *seen* what avocados are!'

'Don't lie to yourself,' Fran said tolerantly. 'You knew perfectly well how much they were when you were eating them.'

Sacha grimaced. 'After ten o'clock at night I lose all my will-power.'

'Indeed,' Fran returned in dry tones.

Sacha threw a cushion at her. 'That isn't what I meant! Come to this party with me tonight and preserve me from the peanuts. They're criminally high on the chart.'

'Take up self-hypnosis. You count down from ten to nought, then picture yourself three stones heavier and repeat monotonously, "I must not touch the peanuts".'

'Oh, do come,' Sacha coaxed. 'Everyone would be thrilled. They all keep asking about you, and there could even be some interesting men there.'

'I'm off men at the moment,' Fran said with a faint smile.

Sacha preserved a tactful silence and she guessed Seth had told her about Grant. She hadn't asked him to keep it to himself and he probably meant well. She had half-expected to hear from him after that revealing kiss, but there hadn't been a word from him either. Possibly just as well. Libby had first claim on him.

She realised Sacha was regarding her enquiringly, and said, 'No, honestly, I just don't feel like a party.'

'Darling, you're becoming an absolute recluse,' Sacha protested. 'It isn't *good* for you.'

'You can't be a recluse when you're surrounded by people for the entire day,' Fran pointed out reasonably. '*Do* get ready and go out, Sacha. All In ask is that if you bring any of them back with you, you keep the music down after one o'clock.'

Sacha admitted defeat and went out later looking exotic and weird, her black hair scraped back so tightly she looked as though she had been scalped, and three brilliant red ostrich feathers stuck into the knot on the back of her head. Her red silk top was scandalously low cut, and Fran surveyed her dispassionately and observed, 'You'll probably get raped.'

Sacha grimaced. 'No chance—Richard's taking me. You haven't met him yet. He's the most utter wimp, but he's filthy rich and he does have this fabulous car.'

Fran laughed, and when she had left, flipped through the records and tapes for something to break the silence. Sacha's taste in music was as way-out as her clothes, and Fran seldom got round to buying anything for herself. She could never remember what they were called, and she baulked at the idea of humming them to the assistant in front of an interested queue as Sacha did quite happily.

She dusted the cigarette ash out of the grooves of a Simon and Garfunkel record, then sorted a paperback from the pile leaning against the wall. Her aunt, she knew, would have been shocked to the core of her methodical soul if she could have seen the flat. Fran preferred more order herself, but she paid only a token contribution towards the astronomical rent. Sacha earned more in a month than she did all year, and she had a generous allowance from her parents besides. All the furniture was hers as well, so it was left how she liked it. She had a large poster proclaiming 'Chaos is Comfortable', on the back of the door. Fran retaliated with one she made herself, saying, 'Squalor is the sign of a disordered mind!' but Sacha only screamed with laughter.

She settled in the corner of the settee with the book, but after half an hour the print began to blur and she laid it down. On the whole she felt reasonably well, but she wasn't a hundred per cent yet and she still tended to tire easily. When the bell rang she started, not sure whether she had actually been to sleep or not, and got up reluctantly to answer it.

It was Grant.

The sight of him jolted through her like an electric shock and she stood there frozen as his initial surprise gave way to conjecture. Finally, he said almost gently, 'Aren't you going to let me in, Fran?'

After a second of indecision she slid the chain free, her fingers fumbling. She was crazy but she couldn't bring herself to slam the door in his face.

He walked in behind her, his eyes straying round the room and taking in her coffee cup and her paperback lying pages down on the arm of the settee. Obviously she was alone, and equally obviously she must be staying here. In her half-stupor when she opened the door she had forgotten she was supposed to be living with Seth. Grant had been expecting to find Sacha.

With a supreme effort of control she made her voice toneless and asked, 'What have you come for?'

'Believe it or not, your address.'

Facing him squarely, she said, 'Why?'

'So I could see you. Why else would I want it?' He paused, examining her. 'You appear to be living here. Didn't it work out with Bernstein?'

Oh God, what did she say to that? Stalling, she told

him, 'I don't think that's a question I want to answer.
And it isn't really anything to do with you, is it Grant?'

Still studying her, he didn't reply at first, then he
said, 'Perhaps—perhaps not.'

Wondering if he was being deliberately enigmatic she
stared back at him, searching his face as frankly as he
had done hers. Irrelevantly she thought she had never
noticed the keen intelligence behind those light eyes
before. Probably because at fourteen she had been too
concerned with the more obvious physical aspects,
though she was more deeply disturbed by him than
ever.

She tightened her stomach muscles, fighting the
sensation, and drew a steadying breath. 'What do you
want?'

'Ah, that's another difficult question,' Grant said
reflectively. 'I don't think the time has come for it yet.'

He took his coat off without being asked and looked
for somewhere to put it. Ashamed of the state of the
room, Fran held her hand out for it. She took it
through to her bedroom and on the way back went into
the kitchen to put the kettle on. Her hands were
trembling so much that she rattled the cups when she
was putting them down, and grains of coffee spilled
from the spoon and scattered across the table. She
watched them form dark brown pools in the water
Sacha had slopped on to the table top.

God, it was humiliating that Grant could reduce her
to this state. Humiliating and stupid, because she
actually knew so little about him that she would have to
ask how he liked his coffee.

Angrily she wiped the table clean and threw the
dishcloth back into the sink, then stood a moment
longer trying to calm herself before she went back into
the lounge.

Grant had his back to her studying their one and

only picture. It was another of Sacha's acquisitions; an original oil painting which she had paid a fortune for, and totally incomprehensible to Fran, who liked to have some inkling of what a picture was meant to be about.

Grant hadn't heard her, so for a moment she could watch him unobserved, her eyes hungrily following the lines of his shoulders and back under the thin, stretched material of his black sweater. As though sensing her presence, he turned suddenly and indicated the painting.

'Yours?'

She shook her head, thinking he knew as little of her as she did of him. 'My taste is for the less esoteric. I go for moonlit seascapes and anything that reminds me of a Constable.' He gave her a faint, unrevealing smile, and she said, 'Do you like your coffee any special way?'

'Fairly strong and without sugar. Otherwise I'm not fussy.'

She gave it him black and he punctiliously remained standing while she cleared a chair of Sacha's jumble and sat down. Then, he demanded abruptly, '*Is* it finished between you and Bernstein?'

'Why are you asking?'

His flash of impatience was quickly hidden but his eyes were steely with purpose when he raised them again. His voice level, he said, 'It was a straight question. Do I get an answer?'

'That depends.'

He raised his brows in enquiry, and she said deliberately, 'How is Julia?'

Instantly his face closed, an impenetrable barrrier coming down between her and his thoughts. After a second of hesitation he said curtly, 'She's fine.'

Turning, he picked up his cup, and Fran said flatly, 'You do feel some sense of guilt, then.'

His head jerked round in a swift movement. 'Yes! But since you couldn't possibly know the cause, what am I meant to infer from that?'

Taken aback by the question and the harshness of his tone, Fran found herself stammering. 'I ... I should have thought it was obvious. After all, she is your wife, and ...'

'Ex-wife!' he interrupted in the same harsh voice.

For a moment everything whirled round her, the shock was so sudden and extreme. She saw him through a haze, his words repeating themselves endlessly in her petrified brain, then his face came into focus again, and still stupefied, she whispered, 'I didn't know ... I had no idea. When ...? Why ...?'

'She left me,' he said, his face unreadable now. 'Three years ago. Didn't your aunt ever tell you?'

Still whispering, she said, 'No.'

To her eternal shame she had hardly ever been back the last few years, and then only for flying visits. And any reference to Grant she had cut off so sharply that her aunt and uncle had ceased to mention him. Probably his divorce had been reported at the time but she had missed it, and there had been nothing since to cause her to wonder. For a celebrity, Grant managed to keep a remarkably low profile in his private life.

She looked up and met his grim stare. Incredibly hardening his voice, he demanded, 'Do you really think I should be here if I was still married?'

Reading condemnation for herself, she retorted, 'How should I know? One can't form judgments of that sort at fourteen!'

As she uttered the words she felt heat rise up in her, a sweat of embarrassment filming her temples at the thought of the memories they must evoke for him as well as for her. She could see now the expression on his face as he realised her action had been no accident, but conscious, sexual provocation. Whether she would have taken fright if she had succeeded in her aim she didn't know, and it scarcely mattered now. It was Grant who had needed protection from her, not the other way round.

There was no possibility that he might regard it as a trivial incident to be lightly forgotten. She had put the fear of God into him with her adolescent passion—forced him to leave his home and the horses and dogs he loved to escape from her. He had been twenty-eight and fully alive to the danger she represented to him. Spurned passion could change without warning to a hatred just as violent in girls of that age. There were countless cases of their fantasies forming the basis for accusations which had ruined men before now. Even when their victims were proved innocent some of the mud would always stick, leaving that lingering doubt which was never completely forgotten.

Oh yes, Grant would remember, as clearly, if not more so, than she did.

She tensed as realisation hit her. Of course he remembered! What else but that memory could have brought him here tonight? She was adult now, not a danger but a promise if that overwhelming physical attraction he held for her had survived the passage of time.

And it had. The knowledge shamed her so that she could hardly bear his eyes on her, hardly bear to look at him in her turn.

He was watching her, whatever thoughts her sharp reply had given rise to hidden behind his impassive expression.

'Let's start again from the beginning,' he said evenly. 'Now we've established that I have single status again, can I repeat the question? Is it over between you and Bernstein?'

In a quandary she wondered how much to tell him. It was unthinkable to admit that even though she believed him to be married she had been so terrified by her own inability to resist him that the whole thing had been an arranged fiction. In the end she took the simplest course and said, 'It's finished.'

'Completely?'

She nodded, and without inflection he said, 'The man's in love with you.'

'Perhaps.'

'Poor devil,' he commented grimly.

Her reply had sounded callous she knew, but there was no explanation she could give without betraying herself. She hadn't known how Seth felt about her. Looking back now she realised there had been signs, but to her it had been nothing but a business partnership that had developed into friendship. They often sat in his office drinking coffee and talking until late in the evening, but when he took her home and tried to kiss her, she'd turned his advances lightly aside. She'd merely thought that he couldn't help trying it on with any attractive girl, and she hadn't wanted their relationship complicated.

When she looked back at Grant his expression was still grim, and with a glance at her yellow jeans he said abruptly, 'Go and put something else on and I'll take you for a meal. It will have to be somewhere that will let me in without a tie, so don't dress up too much.'

Uncertainly, she said, 'I've already eaten. I had something when I got in.'

'We'll go for a drink then.'

His tone was uncompromising, and she saw a sudden gleam of humour in the light eyes. 'If you imagine you can trust yourself to me alone here, Fran, I feel bound to tell you you're mistaken.'

Taken aback by his bluntness she flushed, then felt a

wild excitement surge through her. Hurriedly, she said, 'I'll go and change,' annoyance mixing with the excitement as his laughter followed her.

His dark blue Daimler was parked a little way down the street. As she got in she remarked, 'Quite a change from the Range Rover,' and immediately felt her face colour because it was a reminder of the past again, and of that day neither of them would ever forget. With a kind of despair she reflected that the intervening years might never have been. She still quivered at his nearness, as eager for his touch as that reckless, inviting fourteen-year-old had been.

She wondered what would have happened if Grant hadn't insisted on coming out, and knew she didn't really want to go with him to some hotel or pub where they would be restrained by company. She shied away from what she really wanted, refusing to allow herself the thought, and saw Grant turn his head quickly to look at her. His hand was still on the ignition key and she knew he was as aware of her and what she was feeling as she was of him. She sensed indecision in him for a moment then he switched on the engine and she sighed with an odd mixture of relief and disappointment.

He took her to a wine bar, picking it at random, and they sat at a dimly lit table in a corner and shared a carafe of white wine. It was noisy so that they had to sit close together to hear each other speak, and she asked him about his writing because it seemed the safest topic.

Eyes narrowed in a smile under the thick lashes, he said, 'It's a broad subject. Which particular aspect do you want to know about?'

She shrugged, suddenly feeling hot in her winter-weight cape. 'I don't know, really. I suppose it's just that it's hard for me to think of you as a writer.' She couldn't avoid their mutual background forever so she took the plunge. 'I always think of you in connection with horses and dogs and talk of wheat crops.'

He nodded, still smiling. 'What happened to the little chestnut mare?'

'My uncle had to have her put down. She got rheumatism badly.'

'And there's only one of the three Jack Russells left. She's an old dog now.'

'Which one?'

'Ruff, the runt of the litter. She outlived them all.' For a moment he stared down into his glass, his face withdrawn. 'We're all nine years older. A lot has changed.'

'Particularly for you. Country gentleman to famous playwright.' Driven to utter the words in spite of an inner warning, she said, 'And you've been married in between as well.'

It was the nearest she dared get to a direct question. She had phrased it so that he could ignore it if he wished, but he chose not to. Raising his eyes from the glass, he said, 'You're out of bounds, Fran.'

'I'm sorry,' she muttered. 'I'm being inquisitive.'

He shook his head, leaning back. 'No, that's the wrong word. It implies nosiness and I know it wasn't that.' He paused, turned inward on his own thoughts for a while, then said in a level voice, 'It would be unfair—insulting—to Julia to discuss the reason for the divorce with you, except to say that she was completely innocent. The fault was mine and I deeply regret it, but unfortunately it was one of those things that is impossible to resolve, so . . .'

He raised his shoulders and Fran said quickly, 'Subject closed. It was appallingly bad mannered of me to bring it up.'

She turned away from him and wriggled out of her cape, jealousy knifing through her. She hadn't expected

him to abuse Julia nor to give details of what was
essentially a very private matter, but she had been
totally unprepared for the guilt she could sense behind
his words; the strong loyalty he obviously still felt
towards her.

Even now Julia was blameless, a woman without flaw
he had driven to desert him. She wondered incredulously
what he could have done—what monster could be
hidden under the surface that had made it impossible
for her to stay with him.

Escaping finally from the hot folds of her cape, she
gave it into his extended hand and he took it to a coat
rack. When he returned she had herself under control
again and managed to ask quite naturally, 'When did
you start writing?'

He re-filled their glasses and said absently, 'Oh, it's
something I've always done for my own amusement.
God knows how many first chapters of novels are
hidden away in drawers back home. Television
reception was abysmal in those days and it was
something to do in the long winter evenings. I never
considered it seriously until I went to university, though
you can forget all those newspaper stories about instant
success. I'd spent a hell of a lot of time and done a hell
of a lot of writing before I earned enough to cover the
cost of the typing paper.'

Wryly, Fran said, 'You make me feel humble. I can't
even type.'

'Because you've never needed to,' he pointed out.
'How is the modelling business?'

'Not what it's cracked up to be,' she said
dismissively. 'Over-crowded and not very highly
regarded. Most people equate it with a low IQ.'

'To be fair, I've met one or two who were pretty
dim.'

'There are dim ones in every job, but you can say

you're a typist without it being automatically assumed that you're half-witted or that every pay negotiation is conducted from a horizontal position!'

He flicked her a swift glance. 'Don't get heated. *I* didn't assume it.'

'Then you're in the minority. It does go on, of course, but it doesn't apply to all of us, and personally I prefer to keep work and my private life separate. I was never so . . .'

She broke off what she had been about to add, suddenly aware that she was presenting Grant with a very contradictory picture of herself.

He was watching her with a faintly cynical twist to his mouth, and bluntly he demanded, 'Where does Bernstein fit in then?'

'I . . .' Tongue-tied, she flushed deeply and his expression hardened. Seeing it, she found she was more ashamed of what he believed than what he might guess if she told him the truth.

But it was still difficult to get the words out and she had to force them. Her voice low, she said, 'What Seth said at the hospital, making you think we were living together—it wasn't true . . .' She halted, swallowing as she met Grant's swift frown. 'He'd just been telling me that you'd been round to his office asking questions about me, and he tends to exaggerate everything, I know, but he seemed to think you . . .' She paused again, then went on, 'Anyway, I thought you were still married and I didn't want to get involved in anything, so I asked him to play along—pretend things were serious with us. Seth took it rather further than I intended. He doesn't like half measures.'

'He certainly doesn't,' Grant agreed grimly. He tilted the carafe to see how much was left in and Fran wondered if he would point out that she could simply have said no to any unwelcome suggestion on his part.

He was bound to realise that it had been against herself that she had needed Seth's reinforcement, but he only said, 'So you didn't know I was divorced. Was that the only reason for the double act?'

Evasively, she replied, 'I came tonight,' and he smiled, the quick, brilliant expression she remembered so well.

'My reward for persistence.'

He reached for her hand and balanced it across his palm. 'It wasn't easy to come back, believing what I did.'

Her hand still across his, he began slowly rubbing his thumb round the end of each nail. It set her teeth on edge, like the half pleasurable frisson of a finger run down the spine, and she shivered suddenly with the thought that she could so easily have succeeded in her object and he might never have come back. She whispered, 'I only did it because I thought you were married, Grant. I'm sorry.'

'So am I.' He gripped her fingers, grinding them together so that she winced. 'You caused me weeks of self-destructive mental torture. I've lain awake every night imagining you in bed with him.' He released her hand abruptly and looked up at her. 'Am I pushing you?'

'Yes . . . I don't know.'

She swallowed again, confused because she didn't know what he wanted from her. Not what she had first thought, for in spite of the almost tangible physical tug between them he had deliberately brought her out, away from the empty flat and opportunity. She was puzzled and overwhelmed, projected in too suddenly and too deep. Or was she? Wasn't she prepared to give Grant whatever he wanted? Be whatever he wanted her to be?

Breaking into her thoughts he said, 'It's getting late.

I'd better take you home.' She glanced round to find the place had almost emptied, and he sent her a crooked smile. 'I'm tied up tomorrow with a meeting on scripts, but don't eat when you get in on Thursday. I'll come for you about eight.'

He hadn't asked if she would go out with him, but it never even crossed her mind to resent his calm assumption. What lay in the more distant future she couldn't know, but there was a curious inevitability to what was happening now.

When he drew up outside the flat she looked up at their darkened windows on the first floor and saw Grant follow her gaze. He sat unmoving while she found her key and prepared to get out, and at the last moment, impelled by a fierce yearning, she leaned towards him and whispered, 'Kiss me, Grant.'

He gave a smothered groan and grabbed her hair in one hand, holding her away from him so that he could look into her face.

'What are you trying to do, Fran?' he demanded roughly. 'If I kiss you, you know as well as I do that we'll end up in bed. Are you telling me that's what you want?'

It was, but it seemed too shameless, too wanton, to tell him so without even a preliminary caress or endearment between them. She drew away, and Grant said softly, 'We need to get to know each other, Fran, and it would get in the way—blind us. We shouldn't know what we thought about each other, only what we felt.'

'Yes,' she agreed, matching his quiet tones.

She gave him a quick, tremulous smile and got out of the car, but when she had let herself in through the front door she stood for a moment with her hand against it wondering if he was right. She had never been able to separate her thoughts from her feelings where Grant was concerned, and she couldn't imagine how it could be made any worse.

CHAPTER THREE

SACHA shrieked with envy when Fran told her she was going out with Grant. Her mobile face splitting into a wide grin, she exclaimed, 'Darling, I *told* you he was terribly worried about you! Tell me all about it!'

'There's not a great deal to tell. We went for a drink and he's taking me out for a meal tomorrow.' Seeing the faint enquiry in Sacha's expectant gaze, she added, 'And he's divorced, otherwise I shouldn't be going.'

'It struck me as strange for you,' Sacha said candidly. 'None of my business of course if he hadn't been, but one's liable to get frightfully messy and sordid complications, especially with someone so well known.' She raised her brows. 'Do you want me to be out when you get home?'

'No,' Fran said, colouring. 'I think it might be better if you were here.'

Sacha gave another little scream. 'Is he terribly virile?' She sighed ecstatically. 'Oh, all that lovely masculinity! It makes me drool!'

Nervously, Fran said, 'Sacha, you're to behave yourself and not say anything shocking when he comes. And if you start fluttering your eyelashes at him I'll kill you!'

'He's definitely my type, sweetie, but somehow I don't think I'm his.' The regret in her voice was only half-assumed, and Fran pulled a threatening face at her.

'Go out and catch your own. This one's mine!'

'We're frightfully possessive after only a couple of hours of his company,' Sacha drawled. She looked up from filing her nails and regarded Fran speculatively. 'Unless you were a very precocious little girl.'

41

'In thought, perhaps,' Fran admitted. 'I did have rather a crush on him, but at that age I didn't get the opportunity to extend it to deeds. Actually I was nearly seventeen before I was first kissed, if you can believe it.'

'*God*, darling!' Sacha exclaimed in astonishment. 'I was first kissed in the cloakroom in the infants' school! Though I must confess that at the time I hadn't the remotest idea what people did it for.'

'What made you then?' Fran enquired, amused.

'The grubby little swine had hidden my plimsolls and he wouldn't tell me where they were until I did!'

Fran let out a peal of laughter. 'It doesn't sound as though your first experience was any more stirring than mine.'

With another oblique glance, Sacha said, 'Have you ever been stirred?'

'Not a great deal,' Fran replied shortly.

Sacha held one of her purple talons up in front of her and studied it with absorbed interest. 'Not even by the celebrated writer?'

'Possibly I might have been, but he didn't kiss me.'

Sacha's regard changed to a fixed, bemused stare. 'Life is full of surprises,' she murmured, then twisted round and asked baldly, 'Why?'

'The atmosphere seemed rather too—combustible.'

'But how thrilling! You mean his intentions might be honourable?'

'Sacha, I haven't the remotest idea what his intentions are! Since all he's done so far is take me for a drink, I don't suppose he's got any.'

'Don't be naive, darling,' Sacha said with mild contempt. 'They've all got evil ones.' She wielded the nail file for a moment and surveyed the result, then commented, 'Judging on appearance, I would have said gentlemanly restraint was a teeny bit out of character.'

'Perhaps he's afraid he'd have to find himself another blacksmith if he seduced me,' Fran suggested flippantly. 'My uncle is the only one for miles around back home.'

She saw Sacha's lip curl in derision and suddenly stood up with a jerky movement and went to stand by the fireplace. She had lain awake for hours after Grant left her, puzzled and confused by his rejection of her unspoken offer. Initially she had thought it was what he had come for but he had proved her wrong, so what *had* brought him?

In her own case first love had endured. All the wild longings he had aroused in her in those teen years had only intensified, but a man of twenty-eight didn't feel for a fourteen-year-old what she had felt for him.

It was when he was speaking of Julia that the faint, uneasy suspicion had started to take shape, and she had felt her presence like a ghost at the table, an unwelcome third between them. Grant had revealed regret, remorse, in the way he spoke of her—the woman he had loved and married and shared his life with for six years. The woman he still loved?

And she and Julia were so alike that even all those years ago her uncle had said they could be sisters. So alike that he must be reminded of Julia every time he looked at her. His reaction to her had been too quick and too strong to be merely the product of ordinary physical attraction, and besides, if that had been the case, he would have taken advantage of her willingness. The very fact that he hadn't was confirmation that she was merged in his mind with Julia, for no man would ever dream of treating Julia with anything but the utmost respect. Cynically, Fran reflected that she would bring out chivalry in even the most dedicated womaniser, and for a moment she wondered how Grant had managed to reconcile both of them in his mind. But if feelings were strong enough they overrode everything,

thoughts, reason, common sense, leaving nothing but a
blind response which left no room for anything else.

She went out next day and spent far more than she
could afford on a dress for the evening. It was in soft,
swirling material, patterned in pinks and greys, and
fitting high up to the neck at the front. It wasn't her
usual style, and her long hair didn't look right with it,
but it wasn't until she was pinning it up on the top of
her head that she realised the dress was exactly the kind
of thing Julia wore, and that her hairstyle was almost
identical to Julia's when she had seen her that time in
the theatre.

Arms upraised, she stared at herself, stunned, her
mind too frozen to function when the doorbell rang and
Sacha said obligingly, 'Make sure it's safe, sweetie. I'll
let him in.'

In the mirror, she met Grant's eyes almost fearfully
as he came in through the door. He halted, his smile
fading, then walked up behind her and said, 'Take it
down.'

Too overcome to reply she stood mutely while he felt
in her hair for the pins and removed them, and the
silvery blonde curls tumbled about her shoulders again.
He lifted them in his hands, then let them fall back, and
ordered, 'Leave it like that.'

Fran found she was shaking. She hadn't meant to
copy Julia—the intention had never entered her head,
but she had tried, with her dress and her make-up, to be
the sort of woman she thought Grant admired.
Unconsciously she had made herself into an almost
perfect facsimile of his ex-wife, and for a split second
his eyes had revealed an inner anguish. He had hidden
it quickly, but she knew the memory of that stark
expression would be with her for a long time to come.

Hands trembling, she picked up the comb and ran it
through her hair. It really was too long to wear loose,

and forcing a smile, she said, 'Compromise,' and pulled it forward over one shoulder to form it into a thick, loose plait as she had sometimes worn it when she was young.

With her expensive dress and high heels it now seemed sophisticated, and Grant nodded agreement when she had finished, picking up her cape to slide it on to her shoulders.

Sacha had been watching the by-play intently, aware that it had some significance that was not apparent to her, but her expression changed to one of superior benevolence as she surveyed them both, and grinning, she said, 'Have a lovely time, children.'

'We shall, but no thanks to you,' Grant returned. 'Why the devil didn't you tell me Fran was sharing with you?'

Sacha's eyes widened. 'You never asked, darling,' she said limpidly. 'And besides, I thought you knew. I presumed Seth had sent you.'

'Nothing so simple,' Grant told her, his smile crooked. He propelled Fran ahead of him as he spoke, leaving Sacha to stare after them in frustration, and when they reached the street, Fran said, 'Was that just the instinct of a playwright for a good exit line?'

'Possibly,' he admitted, smiling faintly. 'But I did have a hell of a game finding you. I went round nearly everyone at that bloody party before I eventually got a girl who said she thought you were a friend of Sacha Longraine's. It's an unusual name so I was able to track her down. At the time I didn't even know which hospital they'd taken you to.'

'My aunt and uncle could have given you my address,' Fran said hesitantly.

'They could, but they wouldn't.'

She sent him a glance of swift surprise and he shrugged. 'I asked them for it some time ago, but I was given the impression that I was *persona non grata* where you were concerned. Didn't they ever mention it?'

She shook her head. They may have tried and she'd stopped them, or it could have been before his divorce and they thought they were acting in her best interests in not telling her. They would have been deeply suspicious of any interest on the part of a man in Grant's position.

He reached out and slid a hand down her cheek. When she turned to look at him, he said, 'So I wasn't going to let you get away again when I *had* found you.'

He started the car and put it into drive while she was still going over what his words implied. It was ridiculous that she could love him and yet not know him well enough to be sure of how much he meant by them. But it was too soon to be seeking reassurance from him. He had said himself that they needed time to get to know each other and he was right.

The restaurant he took her to she could never clearly recall afterwards, just as she hardly remembered what they ate or talked about. The food disappeared and plates were removed without smells or tastes impressing themselves on her consciousness.

They talked and smiled and answered each other's questions, drank their wine and their coffee, but it was all dreamlike. Beneath it was the true reality, the mounting tide of awareness consuming them both under the surface. Conversation slowed and died, everything seemed suspended, and Grant said abruptly into the silence, 'Let's go.'

He paid the bill and drove her home through dark, wet streets in the same charged silence. As though mesmerised, Fran watched the rain sliding down the windscreen and being lit up into individual sparkling droplets by the headlights of oncoming cars. When he stopped and switched off the engine she was strained with expectancy.

For a moment neither of them spoke, then he said flatly, 'I was wrong before, wasn't I? We've got to get this out of the way before we can even begin to find out what we think about each other.'

She swallowed and whispered helplessly, 'I don't know, Grant. I don't know anything any more.'

He watched her for a few seconds longer, his hands rigid on the steering wheel, then with a muffled exclamation he reached for her, pulling her against him, his mouth on hers brutal with a stark hunger that jolted all her nerves into wild, uncontrolled response. Twisting against him convulsively she felt his hand thrust her cape aside to find her breast, the hard, hot pressure of his fingers a pleasure and a pain. The sensation made her gasp and she strained towards him even more frantically, searching for a closeness denied them by the confines of the car.

When he lifted his head at last, she was trembling with a desire she made no attempt to hide or control. Grant knew it was there, just as she knew the same passion was raging through him, blinding him to their surroundings and the pain he was inflicting on her with his savage grip. In the quiet, the harsh sound of his breathing mingled with that of hers as they stared at one another in the darkness, oblivious to everything except the overpowering desire driving them both.

Then footsteps rang out on the pavement outside, recalling them. Two teenage girls sauntered by, pausing to giggle as they passed the car, and Grant swore under his breath, watching as they dawdled away with backward glances. When they had gone he pulled her into his arms again and sighed harshly into her hair.

'I could easily have forgotten we're in the bloody car in the street. And you wouldn't have stopped me, would you?'

Fran gave a small, shaken laugh. 'No,' she admitted.

'At least, I don't think so. Perhaps you'd better not put me to the test.'

'You're no help,' he said with wry humour.

His arm tightened and he turned to find her mouth again, but more gently this time. Warned by the previous, violent flare-up of emotion he was holding himself in check, and it was Fran who pressed herself urgently against him, his closeness and the heat of the first embrace still racing her blood.

For a moment he drew away. She gazed up at him and he muttered, 'God, what am I to do with you?' then kissed her again, his hands roving her body under the concealing cape, moulding and caressing through the thin material of her dress.

Impatient of the fine barrier, he reached behind her neck to the fastening, but the long zip stuck only part of the way down, thwarting him, and with a muffled exclamation of frustration he abandoned it and slid his hand beneath the folds of her full skirt. As his palm smoothed up her thigh and his searching fingers encountered the warmth of her flesh she whimpered against his mouth, the stroking, sensual touch sending a shudder of craving through her.

Through the thudding of her pulses she heard him murmuring her name, whispering it over and over again into her hair and her throat in an almost frenzied undertone, then he suddenly wrenched himself away and said roughly, 'This isn't doing either of us any good, is it?' His lips twisted into a smile which was half-grimace, he added, 'Or at least, I know the effect it's having on me!'

She leant her head back against the seat, eyes closed, the breath catching in her throat, and he said questioningly, 'Fran . . .?'

She could only shake her head, and his voice harsh with suppressed emotion, he said, 'Oh God, it's madness, and you're crazy if you agree, but let's get married and sort the rest out afterwards!'

For the space of a second she wondered if she had imagined his words. She turned towards him quickly. He was tense and still, waiting for her answer, and a wild joy sang in her veins. Half-laughing, half-crying, she said, 'I'm crazy, Grant.'

His mouth sought hers, and she returned the kiss with total abandon, her lips already parted for him. After a while he put her away from him and told her brusquely, 'Sit up. We have to talk.'

She nodded and he put a hand on her shoulder, then took hold of her thick plait, slowly twisting it.

'I've got to go to Scotland tomorrow for the filming of a play. I shall be away for ten days, but I'll get a licence before I leave in the morning and we'll get married as soon as I come back. I shall probably need some sort of proof of identity—medical card or driving licence or something.'

'I've got my birth certificate,' Fran offered. 'I think I can find it fairly easily.'

'They can't ask for more than that.' He tugged on her plait then released it. 'Come on—we'll get it now.'

When she got out of the car her legs felt much as they had done when she took her first tentative steps out of bed in hospital, and her hand trembled so much she had difficulty fitting the key into the lock. Grant took it from her, reaching from behind to open the door, then crossed his hands in front of her waist to hold her against him.

The hard pressure made her aware of the strength of his desire, and he bent and put his mouth to the nape of her neck before saying warningly, 'So don't put any more temptation in my way.'

There was laughter in the low, deep tones, but Fran knew he meant it seriously for all that. Nervously, she wondered if he had any idea of how completely inexperienced she was. Probably not. There had been nothing in her response to him to suggest that he was the only man ever to caress and explore her body. When he tried to bring back some measure of control it was she who had done the inciting, offering herself, inviting him to do whatever he wished. Hardly virginal shrinking, she realised, now her blood was cooler.

When they got in, the light was on in the lounge but Sacha had left a note propped on the shelf to say she had gone to bed. Fran read it and caught sight of herself in the mirror as she replaced it. Her eyes were languorous, heavy lidded and darkened, the full curve of her mouth swollen.

Suddenly self-conscious, she said jerkily, 'I'll go and find that certificate. It's in my bedroom somewhere,' and turned away from Grant's penetrating gaze.

As she went by he caught her wrist and pulled her back, studying her face. Unable to meet his scrutiny, she stared at the intricate design of the dark blues and greys in his tie. He put his fist under her chin, gently tilting her head back, and said deliberately, 'In a couple of weeks we shall be married and that's what I want to see.'

He traced his thumb slowly round the shape of her mouth, then slid it inside her bottom lip. She found the movement unexpectedly erotic and he smiled slightly at her changing expression. 'Don't try to hide desire from me. Sex isn't everything, and some people can manage to get along quite happily without it altogether, but I warn you I'm not one of them. To me it matters.'

She wondered fleetingly where he rated love, then dismissed the question. He wanted to marry her, and whatever his reasons they would have to be enough.

She gave him a wavering smile and after a moment he let her go and she went quickly to her bedroom. The birth certificate was more or less where she expected to find it, and when she got back Grant had put the kettle on in her absence and was spooning coffee into the cups. She handed the paper to him and he opened it and glanced at it casually, then gave a wry grimace.

With sharp uneasiness she asked, 'What is it?' and he shrugged.

'We are mad, do you realise that?' He gave a short laugh. 'I didn't know your name was Francesca.'

Fran watched him read through the rest of the document, her uneasiness deepening. He commented, 'So your father was a farmer,' then folded it and slipped it into his inside pocket. 'What happened to your parents?'

'My mother died when I was a few months old, which is why my aunt and uncle took me. He was my father's brother. They couldn't have children so they were happy and it solved a problem for my father. He was killed in an accident with a tractor when I was four. I don't remember him at all.'

He nodded and said musingly, 'Francesca ... unusual, I like it,' then glanced down at her, smiling as he ran his finger down the edge of her cheek and under her jaw. 'But you'll always be Fran.'

She gazed back at him. He was right, they *were* mad, and she *was* crazy to even contemplate spending the rest of her life with him on the basis of one heated exchange of passion. Trying to hide what it cost her to utter the words, she told him, 'You don't need to marry me, Grant.'

Bluntly, he said, 'I know.' He watched the slow flush steal up her face almost with detachment. 'If I asked you now to come back to my apartment, you would.'

He read the admission in her eyes and smiled again, and desperately she asked, 'Then why *are* you marrying me?'

'Perhaps because I'm getting too old for affairs. Leaving a warm bed and getting dressed to go home can be a bit of an anti-climax.'

'No, seriously.'

The kettle boiled as she spoke, rattling the lid, and he turned away from her and unplugged it before replying. He said then, 'All right, seriously, it's too easy to walk out of an affair. I told you before, I'm not letting you get away from me.'

She almost said, 'Julia did,' but the painfully acquired caution prevented her. She was certain that Grant had read the thought all the same. His mouth was set into a hard line as he poured the water into the cups and looked round for the milk. Fran opened the fridge and took a bottle out, and by the time he turned to receive it from her the grim expression had disappeared.

They carried their cups back into the lounge and from unthinking habit, Fran sat in her usual chair. Grant observed drily, 'Prudent, but not necessary. Come here by me.'

Ridiculously shy she went into his outstretched arm and he kissed her lightly. 'I presume your uncle is still refusing to have a phone put in. You'd better write to them as soon as I've fixed the date. Do we invite them?'

Fran hesitated, and said after consideration, 'I don't think so.'

Her aunt in particular would find it disillusioning, she knew. She was a churchgoer of the old school and disapproved of divorce, and it was possible she might even be against the marriage.

Grant showed no surprise, and said, 'If you start collecting your things together here, we can move them into my apartment when I get back. How much of all this is yours?'

'That poster,' Fran said, indicating it.

He read it with a smile, and his glance roaming round the room, remarked, 'Thank God.'

'Sacha feels insecure unless she's surrounded by muddle,' Fran explained lightly. She had cleaned and tidied up to some extent, but the expensive, starkly modern furniture obviously wasn't Grant's choice either.

He was silent, thinking, and she asked, 'What about your mother and stepfather? Will they come?'

'I'll ring her but I doubt it. She won't fly, and it's a long way to travel for a few minutes in a register office.' He raised his eyes to her face. 'It won't be the sort of wedding girls dream of, Fran. Do you mind?'

'No,' she said truthfully. 'I've never had visions of myself floating down the aisle in bridal white.'

With a small shock she realised she had never imagined herself getting married at all. There had been several men in her life, and one or two, she knew, had been on the brink of proposing, but she had never been emotionally involved with any of them. What would have happened if Grant hadn't found her again? Inwardly she shivered, appalled because she knew that unconsciously she might have waited for him for the rest of her life.

She heard him say, 'Has Bernstein got any work lined up for you?' and still wrapped in her thoughts, replied absently, 'No, I haven't done any since I came out of hospital.'

It wasn't until afterwards that she realised he didn't know about her job in the store and by then he was talking of something else. It didn't matter, she reflected. She only had to give a week's notice and she could do that when she went in tomorrow. She suspected that he didn't like the idea of her modelling and wouldn't be keen on a working wife anyway. Possibly he wanted children. The thought sent a quiver through her, but she couldn't ask him yet. Get married first and we'll sort the rest out afterwards, he had said.

She came out of her reverie to find he had undone the end of her plait and was pulling the strands apart and draping them round her shoulders. He said, 'There,' when he had finished, and smiled at her. 'You look about eighteen like that.'

'I'm twenty-three.'

'I know. And I'm thirty-seven.' His face became sombre for a moment. 'Not far off forty, Fran. Does it matter?'

'No,' she replied without hesitation.

'Satisfyingly prompt.'

His eyes roved her face, lingering on her mouth, and he turned her in his arms and lowered her back on to the settee. His lips hovering above hers, he murmured softly, 'But I can promise that I shall be able to cope with you for a good many years to come.'

She was slow to realise his meaning, and he watched her dawning comprehension with amusement as he gradually brought his mouth down on hers, gently invasive at first, then suddenly harder. She felt the sharp change from practised, sensual expertise, to primitive hunger, unthinking and uncontrolled, and reaction flared in her instantly, quickening her breathing and racing her pulse. The pressure of his arms increased until it was painful, then with a sudden movement he rolled on to her.

She gasped as his weight drove the air out of her lungs. Mouths locked together and pinned beneath the hardness of his heavy body she felt suffocated, and she made a sound of protest in her throat.

Hearing it, he raised his head and muttered thickly, 'This is the reason we're getting married, Fran.'

But it isn't my reason, she wanted to cry. Oh, the driving physical force was present in her just as strongly, but it didn't account for the rest of her feelings. The need she felt to be a part of him was the expression of her love, not its source.

Grant drew a deep breath and lifted himself on his hands to look down at her. He was frowning, almost grim, and without pausing to think, she said, 'You don't like the way you feel about me, do you?'

She met his eyes and saw the flicker of surprise there before he said slowly, 'No, I don't.'

'Why?'

Abruptly, he swung his legs down and rested his elbows on his knees, half-turned away from her. She studied his profile, noting the character lines etched in his face during the last nine years, the implacable set of his strong jaw.

He said at last, 'I suppose because I feel you're a weakness in me and I resent it. Everything else about myself I can control, but my feelings for you I can't. These last weeks I haven't been able to stop myself thinking of you, even though I tried. I nearly drove myself insane imagining Bernstein as your lover.' He turned his head to look down at her, then the thick lashes lowered, veiling the intensity in his eyes. 'But don't ever make the mistake of trying to use it against me, Fran. I'm not dependent on you. I would never allow myself to be dependent on anyone.'

Chilled, she asked, 'But . . . why do you resent it so? Isn't it how people *should* feel about each other when they marry?'

When he didn't reply, she said, 'But you've been married before so you know more about it than I do. Is it because of Julia that you feel the way you do?'

'Leave it, Fran,' he ordered harshly.

'How can I leave it? Is there always to be six years of your life that I must never talk about?'

'We'll talk about it one day, but now isn't the time.'

She pushed herself jerkily into a sitting position. 'Then perhaps now isn't the time for us to be getting married either.'

She stood up and turned her back on him to hide the self-inflicted pain in her face. Following her, he gripped her shoulders from behind. His voice hard with determination, he said, 'Perhaps it isn't, but we're going to. We both know how we feel and what's going to happen, whether it's here tonight or in ten days' time.'

'It's not a good enough reason.' Amazingly she sounded calm, no hint of her underlying misery showing in the words. 'Isn't there something in the vows about so long as ye both shall live?'

After a pause, Grant said, 'I have to admit that I don't know the precise wording of the civil ceremony, but it's something to that effect I agree. So?'

She twisted round and silently met his eyes, and he said, 'I shan't be making promises I have no intention of keeping, if that's what you're afraid of.'

'You made them before,' she pointed out.

His face tightened with the withdrawn look she already feared, and he said deliberately, 'Julia left *me*.'

'Yes, I know, but . . .' Ignoring the warning in his bleak expression, she went on, 'Who instigated the divorce?'

Flatly, he replied, 'She did.'

She wondered why she had bothered to ask. She had known it wouldn't be Grant who sought freedom.

'Has she married again?'

She risked a careful glance at him as she voiced the question, but his face was unreadable again. Except for that grim impatience it was only when he was caught off-guard that he betrayed anything, like earlier in the evening when he had first seen her with her hair coiled on the top of her head.

He said, 'No, she isn't married,' then, almost wearily, 'stop digging, Fran. I told you it was my fault—I haven't hidden it from you, but it was something which could only happen once, from one particular set of circumstances.'

'And you're not going to tell me what they were?'

'Not at this moment, no.'

'Was there anyone else . . . involved?'

He hesitated fractionally, the pause so tiny she could almost have imagined it. 'Not in the sense you mean. The divorce was on the grounds of separation.'

He suddenly pulled her against him, his fingers hard on her spine. Rocking her, he touched his lips to her temple. 'It will be all right, darling, believe me! I know what was wrong the first time and I'm not making the same mistake again. I swear there's nothing for you to be afraid of—you above all women.'

She believed him because she so desperately needed to, and looking up quickly caught a flash of tenderness in his eyes. Reassured, she relaxed against him and he kissed her gently and without heat, like a lover who is sated. When he raised his head she smiled at him, and he said, 'So I'll still book the wedding.'

When she nodded he pressed her face against his shoulder for a moment and said, 'I must go soon. I'll ring you from Scotland tomorrow night to tell you the arrangements. I can give you the hotel number then so that you can reach me if you need to.' Feeling in the back pocket of his trousers, he added, 'And I'll give you a spare key to my apartment so you can go in and have a look round while I'm away.'

She took it from him and he watched her put it safely in her bag, then unexpectedly began to laugh, a deep sound of genuine amusement. When Fran raised her brows at him, he ordered, 'Find me a piece of paper I can write on!'

Sorting amongst the untidy litter of bills and envelopes on the shelf for a notepad, she asked, 'What for?' and still laughing, he regarded her quizzically.

'I think I'd better give you the address as well!'

CHAPTER FOUR

FRAN broke the news to Sacha over breakfast, and withdrawing her attention from her muesli, Sacha said carefully, 'Are you sure you aren't being a teeny bit impetuous, darling?'

'Impetuous?' Fran repeated in rueful tones. 'Why wrap it up? Crazy is what you really mean.'

'True,' Sacha agreed with disconcerting candour. She chewed thoughtfully on her muesli for a while. 'You've always been rather a cautious girl until now. True love seems to have taken you remarkably suddenly.'

She left the question hanging delicately in the air and Fran met her astute gaze and shook her head. 'No,' she said. 'There's nothing sudden about it—it's a revival of a very old theme. I can't remember a time when I didn't love him.'

Unsurprised, Sacha said, 'I rather thought as much.' Then went on briskly, 'Well that accounts for your side of it quite satisfactorily. What's the reason for this delightful and unexpected impulsiveness on his part?' Her eyes returned to Fran's face and dwelt for a moment on the faint marks of abrasion round her mouth. 'Apart from the obvious, of course.'

Flushing slightly, Fran asked, 'Is it as obvious as all that?'

'It looks as though he got a little . . . carried away.'

'A little,' Fran affirmed briefly.

Sacha slanted her a sideways glance. 'Does this sudden decision to wed have any particular significance?'

'No,' Fran said, her flush deepening. 'But it's hardly likely that it would have in this day and age.'

'Oh, I don't know,' Sacha returned vaguely. 'There might be one or two left with an old-fashioned quirk of conscience when it comes to virgins, but if it isn't that . . .' Her voice trailed off musingly, then she said, 'Is it just the obvious?'

'I don't know.'

For a moment Fran was tempted to tell her about Julia, but the fear that Sacha's opinion might confirm her own prevented her, and she shrugged and said, 'But he knows he doesn't need to marry me for that.'

Her eyes widening, Sacha drawled, 'Then you're just going to have to wait to find out what his motives are, sweetie.'

Which was hardly comforting, Fran reflected later. Grant had told her that he wanted her and admitted he couldn't keep her out of his mind, but he hadn't told her he loved her and she suspected the omission was deliberate.

He hadn't said what time he would ring her and she was afraid to go for a shower when she got in from work in case she didn't hear the phone over the sound of the running water. She was cooking scrambled egg when it finally went, and abandoning the pan on the draining board she flew to answer it. In response to her breathless, 'Hello?' Grant said, 'I trust you have no other arrangements for a week on Thursday at three o'clock?'

Feeling suddenly weak, Fran sank down on to the chair beside the phone. She realised that until this moment she hadn't quite believed that they were really going to get married. Clutching the receiver tightly, she gave a shaken laugh. 'I'll just check my appointments book to be certain, but I'm reasonably sure I'm free at that time.'

'Good,' Grant said, sounding amused. 'Because I'm not waiting until Friday. Break the news to your aunt and uncle if you want to, but ask them to keep quiet about it. If it should happen to be a slack day for news we could find ourselves being pestered by the press. I've got to stay in London to be on hand until they've finished filming this damned play, so we can't have a honeymoon straight away and they could be a nuisance.'

It was something which hadn't occurred to Fran. She was marrying the Grant she knew of old, the figure in the open-necked shirt and denims or breeches. The handsome, immaculately tailored television personality somehow seemed a different man, unconnected with her. She made a mental note to warn Sacha not to tell anyone, then asked, 'How is the filming going?'

'It isn't at the moment. We're waiting for it to stop raining and praying it doesn't turn to snow. I'm told the scenery is magnificent but all I've seen from my bedroom so far is a curtain of water.'

'What's the hotel like?'

'Gloom and stags' heads and the natives aren't particularly friendly. Not that I blame them. They've probably never come across anything like this crowd before. Film crews are a breed apart anyway, and the cast keep asking the bar for drinks they've never heard of. I'm tolerated because I'm a whisky man and I've got a Scottish grandmother.' His voice altered, the already deep tones lowering. 'I've got a room the size of a barn and a large and very chilly double bed. I should have brought you with me.'

'Delightful,' Fran said. 'You'd like two of us to freeze.'

'You wouldn't,' he said, laughing under his breath. He paused, then said reflectively, 'On second thoughts, perhaps it's better saved for effective central heating. I had a bath when I got in and my system still hasn't recovered from the shock of the temperature in there.

The Scots are a hardy race.' The amusement back in his tone, he said, 'I'll just think of you instead. An occupation which has its drawbacks, but at least now I can indulge in it in a spirit of anticipation.'

He held the mouthpiece closer for his last words, and to her surprise, Fran found herself blushing. Before she could think what to reply, he said, 'I've got a queue breathing impatience behind me—there are no such refinements as phones in the bedrooms—so take this number down in case you need it.' As Fran wrote it on the telephone pad, he added, 'If the weather clears we shall be out all day but you can get me after dark. I'll ring you tomorrow anyway. Round about nine, if that's all right.'

'Right,' she agreed.

There was a short pause, then Grant said softly, 'Goodbye, darling.'

She said, 'Goodbye,' and replacing the receiver slowly, stared at it for a moment. When she was with Grant she could believe that what she was doing was somehow predestined, ordained by the fates. Separated by hundreds of miles it was very different. Grant had called her darling, but she hadn't the confidence to use any endearment in return.

The most ordinary common sense told her they should wait – that she should give Grant time to get rid of that first fierce heat of the physical attraction between them, then they could stand back and view their relationship more calmly.

But she wasn't going to wait, she knew. Warming up her leathery scrambled egg, she acknowledged that she was allowing herself to be rushed headlong into this marriage because she was afraid that if she gave Grant time he would discover that his feelings for her were based on delusion.

Because she wasn't Julia. However alike they might

be on the surface, Grant was going to find that in
character, thought, background, they were completely
different. It was a risk, letting him make the discovery
too late, but the sexual magnetism was real enough, and
instinctively she knew that even if he realised he had
made a mistake he would still try to make the marriage
work. In time he could come to love her for what she
really was. Perhaps not in the way she did, but people
seldom loved equally, and it was enough that she would
be with him.

As Sacha observed, she was normally fairly cautious
but at lunchtime the next day she went out on a reckless
spending spree. For the actual wedding she bought a
white, knitted silk suit with a Greek key pattern in lilac
round the hem. The price would have made her go faint
to even consider it at any other time, but for once she
didn't care, and mentally setting aside only enough
money to pay up her rent to Sacha, she squandered
everything else she possessed.

By the time she had bought some kid shoes to go
with the suit she was already so late that she hadn't got
the nerve to go back into work, so she spent the rest of
the afternoon in places where she had only window
shopped before. Grant was going to have a penniless
bride, she reflected, selecting nightdresses and a négligé
and some wildly expensive scraps of satin and lace to go
beneath the suit. Her credit card probably hadn't been
aired so many times before in its life.

When she got home she put her purchases carefully
away, then went through the rest of her clothes deciding
which to discard and which to keep. When she had
finished she surveyed the garments remaining in her
wardrobe ruefully. There wasn't a great deal.

She went through the things she was giving away
once more, but there was nothing really useful. They
were young, throw-away fashion clothes, some of them

more trendy than becoming, eye-catching, but not in a way Grant would appreciate. He moved in different circles.

Just how different was brought home to her later when she stood hesitantly in the doorway of his apartment. Feeling like an intruder she advanced slowly into the main room, cringing inwardly as she compared it with Sacha's flat. No wonder he had said, 'Thank God,' when she told him only the poster was hers.

For a moment she felt oppressed and had the urge to turn tail and slam the door behind her. It would be ridiculous. In a few days she would be living here—it would be her home. She tried to imagine herself vacuuming the dull gold carpet and fastening the long curtains back with their elegant sashes. She tried but she couldn't. It was all too far removed from everything she was used to. Sacha's slightly grubby clutter seemed comfortingly friendly as she gazed round at the watered silk wallpaper and graceful, antique furniture.

Attempting to conquer her dismay she went back into the hall and opened another door into what proved to be Grant's bedroom. Grant's and hers, she told herself, more at ease because everything in here was modern from the kingsize bed to the raked pile of the oatmeal carpet. Her eyes scanned round then returned to the bed she would be sharing with him. The prospect brought a clutch of desire, overlaid with nervousness. Which side would she sleep?

Which side had Julia slept?

Overwhelmed by a sudden sickness she opened the drawers and doors of the cupboards built into the headboard. They only contained books and notebooks and a couple of folded newspapers with half-finished crosswords. There was nothing feminine in either of them.

Quickly she went through the rest of the room and

sat on the bed a few minutes later feeling the
overpowering surge of revulsion fade. There was
nothing anywhere. If Julia had ever been in this room,
every single sign of her presence had been removed.

There was bound to be another bedroom though.
Returning to the hall she pushed open the next door
and heard her own sigh of relief as she saw it had been
made into a study. Grant's typewriter sat on a desk
near the window, a row of well-used reference books on
a shelf beside it.

It was all very tidy and ordered, and she carefully
closed the door again as she went out. There was a
bathroom next door, and at the far end of the hall,
the large kitchen, expensively fitted out but bare. She
could find only the minimum of cooking utensils—no
pastry bowl or rolling pin or anything of that nature.
A small utility room led off it, and pausing in the
doorway, Fran was finally convinced. There was no
washing machine. The plumbing was there for one,
the red-and-black hoses connected to taps, but the
space was empty.

Julia had never been here. Even if Grant had gone
through the apartment and deliberately eradicated
every trace of her, he wouldn't go to the length of
throwing out a washing machine and Julia wouldn't
have lived here without one.

Such was the strength of Fran's relief that her legs
felt weak and she realised she had been rigid with
tension from the moment of entering the apartment.
She decided to make herself a cup of coffee, but it
wasn't until she was sitting with it at the kitchen table
that full realisation hit her.

Julia had never lived here—Grant must have
acquired the apartment after she left him—but this
wasn't his home. Home was the sandstone house up on
the hill, and before long he would want to go back.

Unreasoning panic filled her but she fought it down. It wouldn't be yet. They would have some time here first, probably not returning until late spring, and surely by then she would have built up her own relationship with Grant and the spectre of Julia would no longer be so threatening?

The rest of the time before he came back passed too quickly and too slowly by turn. She had written to her aunt and uncle, endorsing secrecy and giving the reason, but in spite of her aunt's known aversion to the telephone she was hardly surprised to receive a call from her the following day.

She heard the pips with a sense of resignation. They seemed to go endlessly, and she could imagine her aunt at the other end, nerving herself to put the money in. When they finally ceased, the breathless, over-loud voice at the other end said, 'Fran, is that you?'

'Yes, Aunt Beth,' she said reassuringly. 'It's very brave of you to ring.'

'Well, I had to! I just couldn't believe what you wrote in your letter! You've never said a word about Mr Mercier before. Your uncle and I had no idea!'

'We decided rather suddenly,' Fran told her apologetically. 'He came to see me in hospital after I had my appendix out and it all started from there.'

Her aunt's appalled tones came clearly over the line. 'But Fran, that's not long enough to be marrying him!' There was a short pause and she added accusingly, 'And why mustn't we tell anyone?'

'I haven't been doing anything I shouldn't, Aunt, if that's what you're thinking.'

'I'm glad to hear it,' her aunt returned tartly. 'But it's what everyone here is bound to think. All the neighbours will naturally wonder why we never mentioned it, our own niece marrying Mr Mercier.'

'All right, you can tell them,' Fran said with an

inward sigh. It would be a nuisance if the news got out, but it was unfair to cause embarrassment needlessly.

'Besides,' her aunt went on, 'well, there's bound to be talk anyway. It's going to be difficult for you. Have you thought about that?'

'Difficult in what way?'

'He's been married before.' Disapproval showed plainly in her voice before it was replaced by discomfort. 'His first wife was very highly thought of round here—she did a lot of good, and her father being a Brigadier, people could respect her. Your uncle and I are just ordinary folk and there are bound to be some who won't accept you in her place.'

'I'm not expecting to be treated any differently by the people I grew up with, just because I shall be married to Grant.'

'It isn't only that ...' Her aunt paused, her discomfort showing plainly now. She went on with a rush, 'It's bound to cause a lot of talk, you and she being so much alike.'

'What can they say except that we are?' Fran returned lightly. The pause this time was so long that she added, 'Are you still there?'

'Yes,' her aunt said at last. As she became more used to the phone her voice had resumed its normal pitch. 'But folk can add two and two, or at least they think they can.' Before Fran could question her she said hurriedly, 'Dora Matthews for one. You're going to get trouble there, because she won't welcome you and that's a fact. She was devoted to his first wife—absolutely devoted.'

Fran felt despair begin to creep over her. Mrs Matthews had reigned as housekeeper for over twenty years and wouldn't easily be dislodged. The despair deepened as she wondered what it was about Julia that seemed to inspire devotion in everyone. Surely no mortal could be so completely perfect? There must be a flaw in her somewhere.

Concerned and fretful, her aunt said, 'Oh Fran, are you sure you know what you're doing? It's all too quick! Wait a bit longer. Come home for a while and talk about it. Be certain.'

It was insanely quick, but Fran didn't dare wait. Steadily, she said, 'I love him, Aunt Beth.'

A faint sigh gusted down the line. 'Folk always think that, or nobody would get married in the first place. There are plenty find they were mistaken.'

She didn't add that Grant was one of them, but Fran knew it was what she meant. It was apparent he had fallen from grace with the divorce. Making her tone bantering, she said, 'Stop being so gloomy or I shall wish you'd never rung.'

'Don't say that! It's just that it was such a shock when we got your letter. I never dreamt of such a thing, and naturally I can't help being worried when it's all so sudden.'

'But it's not as though I was marrying someone you didn't know.'

'I'm not sure I wouldn't be happier if you were.'

Fran stiffened. 'Aunt Beth, please!' she protested.

'Well, you've got to face the fact that if his wife left him he gave her good cause—she wasn't the sort to go off over nothing. Has he told you why she did, I wonder?'

'No,' Fran said. The word wouldn't come out at the first attempt and she had to clear her throat and say it again. 'He told me he deeply regretted it, but it was something which couldn't be put right.'

'Oh, he was sorry enough, I grant you, and there's no doubt he did his best to make amends, but it's too easy to say you're sorry afterwards. It's no excuse.' Grudgingly, she added, 'Even Dora admits he couldn't do enough, trying to make it up to her, but that's what I'm saying, Fran! If she wouldn't stay after all he did to try to persuade her, then it must have been something terrible! Dora said it would break your heart to see how unhappy she was, crying all the time when he wasn't about.'

Tonelessly, Fran observed, 'It sounds to me as though Dora Matthews said altogether too much. There's such a thing as loyalty to the person who pays your wages as well.'

'She perhaps says too much at times,' her aunt agreed uncomfortably. 'But she could tell a lot more if she chose to, and she doesn't make things up, nor she doesn't deny he took it very hard when she went—very hard.'

Fran found she was gripping the phone until her nails dug into her thumb. She let herself slowly down on to the chair by the wall. She didn't want to listen—didn't want to know. With all her heart she wished her aunt had never rung, but still she found herself saying, 'It's something in his favour that he *was* sorry.'

'That's as may be, but he wasn't all that long getting over it.'

'How do you know that?' Fran asked automatically. She didn't really want to know. She wanted time and quiet to assimilate all the other things she had learned, without having more added to them.

A note of defiance creeping into her voice, her aunt said, 'He came round here asking for your address but I didn't think it right to give it to him. I was thankful I hadn't afterwards when he started having women up at that house. Actresses, some of them were.'

She might just as well have said harlots, Fran thought. She had an insane desire to laugh as she imagined how her aunt would have reacted to the information that her own niece had decided to go in for nude modelling.

Her tone censorious, her aunt continued, 'I suppose if you're charitable you could say it was his way of trying to forget—I've heard some that held it was—but in my opinion it's no way to behave whatever the reason.'

Curiously unaffected by the last revelation, Fran did laugh. 'I'll make sure he doesn't take any up there in the future.'

There was a silence. 'You *are* going to marry him, then?'

'Yes.' Fran heard the sigh from the other end and said gently, 'Wish me happy.'

'Oh, I do, Fran.' Her aunt began to cry noisily. 'You know I do. It's only that I was so worried.'

'Then stop worrying and be nice to Grant when we come to see you.'

She made her goodbyes cheerful, but afterwards Fran sat for a long time unmoving, her blind gaze fixed on the opposite wall. Nothing was really changed, she assured herself, she hadn't learned anything new. It was just having her fear confirmed that had shaken her so badly. It was one thing to suspect, but knowing was different, and she wished desperately that she was already married to Grant—safely committed in case something else happened to highlight the folly of what she was doing.

Once she had worked out her notice the days seemed to drag by. With too much leisure for thought and uncertainty she could hear her voice growing more and more stilted each time Grant rang her. On one occasion he asked her sharply if there was anything the matter, but she couldn't tell him she was afraid that away from her he might have come to his senses. He had asked her to marry him in a blaze of frustrated passion—not the best time for a normally intelligent, clear-thinking man to commit himself, and in a later, calmer frame of mind he must question his sanity just as she was doing.

Because of delays caused by the weather he was now due back on the Tuesday. In a fresh frenzy of nerves she was waiting for him to ring to say he was home when he arrived at the flat. She went to the door impatiently, afraid that the phone might go while she was answering it, and stood speechless and rooted to the spot when she saw him.

Without a word he pulled her into his arms. For a while he just held her, then he turned his head to seek her mouth, parting her lips with an urgent, physical hunger, and feeling the rapid rise of her own response, Fran wondered dazedly what it was that made this one man different for her—what chemistry was present in him which the others lacked, and which something in her own body recognised and stretched out to meet.

He kissed her until she was mindless, then raised his head and demanded roughly, 'Has that disposed of your doubts?'

'Yes,' she admitted with a small laugh. 'And butterflies and cold feet and every other description you can think of. I've had them all.'

'Brought on by well-meaning friends and relatives?'

'You can't blame them.'

'Sitting alone in that bloody cold bedroom I did. I knew someone had been getting to work on you.'

His eyes were narrowed, and she was suddenly afraid he might question her on what her aunt had said. To divert him she asked quickly, 'Didn't you have any doubts of your own?'

For a moment his hands roved her arms and shoulders, almost as though he was unaware of his own actions, then he said, 'I know what I feel.'

He hadn't answered her question and she looked up at him quickly. His face was set in lines of sensuality, the nostrils flared, and she thought silently, 'And I know what I feel as well,' but she couldn't tell him because their emotions were different. Even now, with their wedding day so close, he still hadn't said he loved her.

Standing in front of the registrar two days later, Fran wondered if he had ever before married a couple in such obvious and indecent haste to get the ceremony over and done with. Sacha was enormously entertained, but the two clerks, summoned to act as witnesses, tried to pretend they had noticed nothing unusual in the atmosphere and stared at the flower arrangements flanking the table.

Only the registrar seemed unaffected, his measured tones slightly monotonous from frequent repetition of the words. Washed in disbelief that this was actually happening, Fran scarcely heard what he was saying, and she had to concentrate her attention to make the correct responses.

Vaguely she thought it was odd to hear Grant's full name, Charles Grantham Mercier—she hadn't known it was his second name, nor that it was short for Grantham. But then he hadn't known hers was Francesca either, and for a second she faltered in her responses and felt the registrar's eyes on her.

It was over almost before she realised—she had signed her single name for the last time and they were husband and wife. Grant's fingers gripped hers, but his lips barely brushed her mouth in the conventional kiss. From even that brief contact she felt the suppressed desire in him, and she coloured when he leaned over and muttered, 'Now the rites are over, let's get out of here.'

There was only one bored photographer lounging against the wall outside, and he was so bemused by Sacha's purple outfit that he barely glanced at Grant and herself as they threaded their way through a large group of arrivals. Safe in the car, Fran let out a sigh of relief, and Grant said with satisfaction, 'I never thought we'd manage to brush through that unobserved.' He turned to grin at Sacha in the seat behind him. 'Thanks to the distraction.'

Sacha made a disclaiming gesture, and Fran reflected that her aunt's traditional soul would have been outraged had she been present. She suffered a twinge of conscience at the thought. Probably she had been looking forward to a white wedding in the village church, with bridesmaids and flowers and sentimental tears as they went off on their honeymoon. Certainly she would never have imagined this rushed, irreverent ceremony and a prompt return to Grant's apartment afterwards.

They dropped Sacha off on their way. As she disappeared with an airy, 'I'll see you when you surface, darlings,' Fran glanced up at what had been her bedroom window until only hours before and felt a rush of fright.

Gazing round Grant's apartment while she waited for him to put the car away, she told herself that this was now her home. Dusk was beginning to close in so she went into the lounge and switched on the lights, wondering how long it would be before all this was as familiar to her as Sacha's flat. It didn't feel like home yet. Things still caught her attention which she hadn't noticed before, and she didn't know any of the titles in the long rows of bookshelves, or what kind of music was stored in the cabinet that concealed a bank of stereo equipment.

Smitten by nerves again, she realised her hands were trembling and pressed them to her sides. She couldn't just be standing in the middle of the room when Grant came in. Drawing the curtains, she slipped off her jacket and went into the kitchen to switch the kettle on.

It sang and burbled noisily as it neared boiling point so that she didn't hear Grant until he was behind her, and she let out an exclamation of fright as his arms closed round her.

Silently he leaned forward and switched the kettle off again, then slowly turned her and brought his mouth down on hers. Instantly all the damped-down passion of the day flared between them, and he deepened the kiss, forcing her hard against the cupboard with the pressure of his body. Her own arms tightened round him in fierce response and he started to lift her silk top then paused, and his voice thick with urgency, said against her mouth, 'Come into the bedroom and I'll get you out of these properly.'

Swinging her round, he propelled her ahead of him into the fading light in the large room. The bed was tinged with pink from the winter sunset, and she checked, looking at it, then stepped deliberately out of her shoes and turned back to face him. He began to undress her, swearing and laughing under his breath when a hook resisted him, and pausing as he discarded each garment to run his hands over her skin and press his mouth to the flesh he had laid bare. But the laughter died when she stood naked before him. His gaze travelled slowly over her, seeming to touch her as he studied her, the intensity of the desire in his taut expression springing into life a leaping, half-fearful excitement.

She trembled, the quiver starting low in her stomach and spreading through her, and he suddenly pulled her down on to the bed, kissing her and returning to kiss her again as he stripped off his own clothes and came down beside her. Half underneath him, held against the hard length of his body, all the pent-up yearning of years flooded through her in a tidal wave of heated desire. His lips on her breast sent a current along nerves she hadn't known existed, the sensation so piercingly intense it seemed to burn through her flesh. On fire, she writhed, trying to pull free from the tug of his mouth and his erotic, invasive caresses, some instinct warning her that the agonising, spiralling need could build up and spill over unless she checked him.

He whispered questioningly, 'Fran?' as she reached down to stay his hand, and in reply she twisted against him, her action more explicit than words. For a moment he held back. His voice unsteady, he breathed, 'Fran, you're trying to go too fast, darling—you could be left out in limbo,' but she shook her head in frantic denial, the hunger to feel him within her so desperate she no longer cared what she might be betraying of herself.

Half-sobbing, she dug her fingers into his hips to pull him towards her, and with inborn sureness rose to meet him as he covered her. Braced for his invasion she realised he controlled that first movement, searching her face for any sign of protest or distress, but when it came it was no more than a fleeting discomfort, lost in the wonder of greater sensation, and the only thing to be read in her eyes was a naked desire that dissolved the last of his restraint.

Passion unleashed, his arms reached beneath her, locking her up to him, and she thought dazedly that this was what she had craved for all her adult life—this fierce, violent coming together that for a while made him a part of her. Then she was no longer capable of thought, her only consciousness that of the driving force impelling her onward and upward to the rending culmination, the height of all human experience.

She lay for a long time afterwards, limp and still in his close embrace, exhausted by the savage spending of emotion. Finally he eased away and she felt his faint, sighing breath on her shoulder before he turned her face up to meet his gaze.

She stared back at him, straining to see his expression in the last of the light, and his voice low and uneven, he said, 'That was what I dreamed of, Fran, in that barn of a room in Scotland.' He laughed suddenly, a short sound laced with self-derision. 'Waking and sleeping, it's all I've thought of since the night I kissed you. I knew then what you'd be like.'

She should have been filled with happiness because she'd lived up to his hopes and he wasn't disappointed in her, but instead, inexplicably, she wanted to cry. The slow descent from that fevered pinnacle of emotion had brought an emptiness in its wake, leaving her confused and strangely forlorn. She wanted Grant to hold her and tell her he loved her, to kiss her without passion to show she meant more to him than the physical obsession which was all he ever admitted to. Lying beside him now, freed from the compulsion of her own desire, she felt more like a mistress to him than a wife. And yet he had turned down that offer when innate wisdom had forced her to make it.

She cut off the thought, wondering how she could persist in deluding herself even now. Grant didn't want an affair, he wanted the substitute he had made of her in his mind. She had known that this afternoon when he slipped the ring on to her finger. She had accepted it then and she must accept it now, but she knew all the same that she had hoped that with the act of loving he would reveal some deeper, different feeling for her. Something which was for her alone.

Slow tears formed but she restrained them with her lids and turned to press her forehead against his chest. He ran his hand down the side of her face, then continued down gently over her throat and the curves of her body. She felt his fingers pause as they encountered the ridged scar on the side of her stomach, and half under his breath he exclaimed, 'God, I'd forgotten about that!'

Reaching over her he switched on the light and frowningly studied the red line which disfigured her skin. 'Have I done any damage?'

Fran shook her head. 'The surgeon said I could do what I liked as long as I didn't try to lift any pianos in the next two or three months.'

Still frowning, he demanded bluntly, 'Does that include getting pregnant?'

'No.' She coloured slightly, and at the back of her mind thought his enquiry had come a little late. 'I checked with my own doctor and he said I wouldn't come apart at the seams but it would be better to wait a while.' Meeting his swift glance of interrogation, she added, 'But it's all right—it won't happen.'

He continued to regard her, his expression unfathomable, then nodded and traced his fingers over the puckered skin. 'It looks as though he operated with a kitchen knife. I thought they could do it without leaving much of a mark nowadays.'

'Usually, but there was some infection and it didn't heal very well. Do you mind?'

'Yes and no. If you mean does it affect me, no of course not, but aesthetically I hate to see perfection marred.'

So at least she was a perfect body to him if nothing else. She closed her eyes and heard him laugh suddenly, saying, 'Anyway, you're not the only one scarred.'

Her eyes flew open again, and still laughing he turned his shoulder towards her, indicating the teeth marks and the darkening bruise on his skin.

She stared at it, horrified and embarrassed, and his voice light with mockery, he said, 'Perhaps it's just as well we didn't go to some exotic foreign resort for a honeymoon. Who knows what other damage I might be exhibiting on the beach by the end of a fortnight.'

Fran was speechless, shaken to find she had no conscious memory of inflicting the bruise, and he smiled slightly and flicked her nose. 'Forget it—I could have defended myself.' He watched her eyes slide guiltily away from his shoulder, and added, 'Though it might help to know if it's a habit of yours, because if it is I shall need to.'

It took a second for his real question to register, and for her to realise he was asking if she had been a virgin. He wasn't sure. With some women it would be beyond doubt, but he knew that initial pain, or the lack of it, wasn't an infallible guide.

Secure in his love she would have told him what she knew he wanted to hear, but a sudden resentment held her back. That, and the knowledge that it would tell him too much about her feelings for him if he learned that her only experience was the one they had so recently shared. For years his image had come between her and every man she had gone out with, banishing whatever flickering interest they aroused almost before it had begun. The memory of him had kept her untouched, emotionally as well as physically, but Grant brought to their own marriage the memories of a previous one, and of the countless times he had held another woman's naked body under him in that most intimate of all embraces.

Jealousy surged through her with the thought, almost choking her. She turned her face into the pillow, afraid of betraying it, and he said, 'Fran . . .?' then broke off.

There was an odd note in his deep voice, and she felt herself weaken. Even if he hadn't been married, she would still be far from the first to know what it was like to lie beneath him and feel him lose himself in her. He was thirty-seven and she had always known that he was deeply sensual. It was an aura he gave off unconsciously, something she had responded to from the depths of her own nature, and which had given the added spice of danger to her adolescent pursuit of him. But while strong sexual attraction was something she had only ever experienced with him, men were less emotional, more physical in their attitude to sex, and there would have been a good many other woman before her anyway.

But strangely, the others she didn't mind. Only Julia.

CHAPTER FIVE

FOR a while neither of them spoke, and Fran was aware of an irrational sense of guilt. She knew Grant had picked up the lightning change in her expression as she realised what he was asking, and as far as he was concerned there was only one conclusion to be drawn from her silence. Already she regretted it but the moment had passed, and explanation now would take her into forbidden territory.

He sat up, grimacing as he ran his hand over the slick of sweat on the back of his neck, then turned to look down at her, and laughing under his breath, muttered, 'Who needs central heating?'

Fran watched as he reached for a towelling robe and wrapped it round himself before crossing the room to close the curtains against the winter dark. So he had accepted her silence for what it seemed and his manner implied that it didn't matter to him. Apparently he didn't care if she had been to bed with a dozen other men.

Perversely, his tolerance made her angry. For a moment she was gripped again by that fierce sense of betrayal she had felt when she learned he was married, but then logic reasserted itself. Grant knew nothing of the wild passion she had nursed all these years. Along with most people he would presume that by twenty-three she would have been sufficiently attracted to succumb to one man at least.

Her mood swung round abruptly as she recalled the scene she and Seth had played out for him at the hospital, and paralysing fright flooded her at the thought that but for that same tolerance she wouldn't be here now. Weak with thankfulness she rubbed the unfamiliar band of her wedding ring and rolled on her side to follow him with her eyes as he moved towards the door.

He paused to look back at her, smiling faintly at her questioning gaze. 'I'm not going far. Just to have a quick shower and make us a drink. I'll leave you this bathroom if you like.'

She nodded and he studied her for a moment before he went out. The deliberate scrutiny sent a kick of desire through her, catching in her stomach like the heart-stopping physical lurch of extreme fear. The strength and unexpectedness of it dismayed her, and swinging her feet to the floor she wondered if it was normal to react again so violently so soon.

There was no way of knowing, and she shrugged and stood up stiffly, conscious as she did so of the strain in the unaccustomed muscles of her hips and upper thighs. To ease it she ran a bath instead of showering, and emerged from the bathroom still faintly damp to find Grant leaning back against the padded bedhead drinking coffee.

Grinning lazily, he indicated her mug on the table on the far side. 'I'm establishing territories. That's your half.'

'Thank you,' she retorted. 'Fortunately I don't have a preference.'

She tightened the belt of her robe as she spoke and sat on the bed with her back to him. With difficulty she had kept a sharp note from her voice and kept her comment light. It was true she had no preference—she had always slept alone so it was unlikely that she would have, and Grant hadn't realised that his remark was in any way revealing.

Were all second wives so acutely sensitive to every

unconscious reference to a past which had been shared with someone else? Probably. But even as she tried to convince herself she knew that her own case differed from most. Few successors would carry, as she did, the memory of that tortured expression in Grant's eyes when she had unknowingly turned herself into a replica of Julia.

Deliberately she erased the picture from her mind and began to drink her coffee, but an uneasy fear persisted. Inevitably Grant would compare them, and who could live up to Julia? Except perhaps in one area, she thought, with a tiny spurt of hope. No one could really know what anyone else was like behind their public face, but somehow it was impossible to imagine the restrained, impeccably behaved Julia responding equally to the strength of passion Grant displayed. And it was something he openly declared was important to him. If it was her only advantage, there at least, Fran vowed, he should not compare and find her wanting.

She raised the mug to her lips again, but her movements stilled when he slid his hand under her hair, his fingers slowly caressing her nape. His touch was delicate, lingering, and her whole being quickened. She was suddenly conscious of her heartbeat and breathing and the thudding of her pulse—all things which her body normally performed for her, waking and sleeping, without her ever thinking of them.

So acute was her awareness that even her scalp tightened, and his fingers checked, picking up the tiny, almost imperceptible movement. He murmured softly, 'Gratifying!' and leaned forward to remove the mug from her grasp and replace it on the table. The action brought the wall of his chest hard against her back, and she felt rather than heard his laughter as he added, 'I'll make you another one later.'

Turning, she met his eyes, inches from her own. They

still gleamed with amusement, but the clear, light colour had darkened, and reading their unmistakable message, she snatched a shallow breath. For a moment he stared at her, his hands tightening on her shoulders, then he slid the wrap away from her, disentangling himself from the sleeves of his own robe as he pulled her down with him on the bed. Head lowered to find her mouth, he whispered, 'And this time, my darling, we're going to take it slowly.'

But this time she knew just what it was that her inflamed senses craved. The slide of his mouth across hers was a gentle torment, giving more frustration than pleasure because it was not enough. With an inarticulate sound she dug her nails into the flesh over his ribs and heard him laugh before he transferred his lips to her breasts. They seemed to grow heavy, the nipples tumid in the encompassing heat of his mouth, and she felt herself descend again into that mindless abandonment where nothing mattered except that he should free her from the racking need he induced.

Through the pounding of her blood she heard him whispering, 'Easy . . . easy, darling . . .' soothing her, calming with words and gentling touch, but she was beyond the reach of reason, lost to all restraint.

Hazily, she was aware of him gazing at her, eyes narrowed beneath the black lashes, then he drew a deep breath and brought his mouth down on hers with deliberate, sensual invasion. The hands which before had sought to quieten, now moved on her with calculated arousal, so that she felt the muscles deep within her begin to contract and tighten.

Twisting, she tried to escape him, but he held her down, one leg clamped across hers, and when she finally wrenched her mouth free to cry out in protest, to beg him to stop before it was too late, he told her urgently, 'Let go, darling!—let it happen!'

Once more she struggled to break free, but she was helpless in his grip, powerless against his unrelenting expertise, and the inexorable gathering tide she could no longer contain rose up and flooded through her.

As it receded and finally died away she lay with her eyes tightly closed, feeling raw and exposed because she knew he was watching her—had witnessed her with every civilised veneer stripped away.

She felt his lips brush hers, then he said, 'Fran?' and unwillingly she raised her lashes to meet his comprehending gaze. 'That's how I wanted to see you,' he told her. 'Don't try to hide it from me.' He watched her for a moment, smiling faintly as her expression relaxed. 'Some people will only make love in the dark because they're too repressed to reveal themselves, but I'm sorry for them. Seeing what I make you feel is part of the pleasure.'

He smoothed his palm lightly backwards and forwards across her stomach, then lowered himself down beside her again. Sliding his arm under her, he suddenly gave a low laugh, and replying to the question in her eyes, asserted softly, 'And this time, my hot-blooded wife, we *are* going to take it slowly.'

He was an expert lover—even in her inexperience she realised that. The blinding urgency banished, she could appreciate the arts he practised, raising her to a level where she could luxuriate in the response he aroused, then checking her, letting desire build up, yet skilfully holding it short of the point where it became all consuming.

He was totally free from inhibition himself, openly displaying the sensual pleasure he took in exploring and kissing her, and gradually the last of her constraint was eased away. Curbing his own desire he seemed absorbed in the unhurried play, content for the moment to watch the small, receptive movements she made in response to his touch. He made no demands on her, but remembering her vow that he should not find her wanting, she overcame her first hesitancy and returned his caresses, astonishing herself with her temerity.

For a second his eyes narrowed. He regarded her with a curiously assessing look, then bent over her again, and because she was completely unversed she was startled into betraying shock. He felt her stunned recoil from the contact of his mouth, and raising his head, observed with a kind of savage satisfaction, 'Not quite so experienced after all!'

His action and the unexpected note in his voice lifted her abruptly out of her state of warm compliance. Briefly she felt a prickle of warning, but then he began to caress her more urgently, and she forgot it in the fierce heat which coursed through her as the weight and power of his body overcame her.

In the aftermath this time, he brought her all the tenderness she yearned for. Held in his arms, his lips against her hair, she was unutterably happy, totally content as she drifted towards a sleep which carried her into the night.

It was broken when she stirred in response to a slow, insistent caress in the small of her back. When her movement revealed that she was awake, Grant pulled her towards him to demonstrate his arousal, but she grumbled sleepily and he laughed and slackened his hold.

'Not interested?'

She repeated her mumbled demur, burrowing her head under his arm, and he laughed again, softly, and whispered, 'Shall I make you interested?'

Something stirred faintly in her, but she was too drugged by tiredness, and he ceased his caresses and let his hand rest loosely on her hip. She heaved a sigh and slid a languid arm round him, and amusement mixed with the desire in his voice, he said, 'Go back to sleep then—I'll let you off this time,' then added, his mouth brushing her cheek, 'but only until morning.'

And in the morning she awoke to the touch of his hands and lips and an instant, fierce desire.

Afterwards he lay with his head propped on his hand as his eyes moved over her, and rubbing a hand round his darkened chin, commented wryly, 'I don't think either of us could appear with much credit on a beach at the moment.'

She looked down at herself to where her fine skin was roughened by his blue-black growth of beard, the red weals showing clearly. Accusingly, she said, 'Monster!' and he grinned.

'I normally shave twice a day, but last night I was distracted. I forgot.'

'I'll take care to remind you in the future!'

Still grinning, he retorted, 'And I'll get your teeth blunted.' He glanced at his shoulder and she saw that in one place she had slightly broken the skin. He rubbed it and winced. 'Fortunately I'm covered by anti-tetanus injections for the next two years. The mind retreats from the thought of trying to explain it away to some supercilious nurse.'

For a moment she thought he was serious, then she saw his mocking expression and smiled back at him. 'You mean modesty forbids the truth?'

'Oh, yes.' He leaned over her and touched his tongue to one of her nipples, causing her to catch her breath. 'Even at the risk of being suspected of forcing my attentions on some unwilling female, how could I admit that I reduce my wife to such a demented state of passion ...' He stopped, his voice thickening, then suddenly laughed and pushed himself upright again. 'God, I don't think I've got the strength until I've had some food. Do you realise we haven't eaten since lunchtime yesterday? I hope you can cook.'

'As long as you're not too fussy. I eat my own cooking quite happily.'

He raised his brows. 'Two eggs, lightly fried? Bacon, sausage, mushrooms, tomatoes?'

She swung her feet to the floor with a grimace. 'It's disgusting to even talk about things like that at this hour in the morning. Orange juice and toast.'

He pulled her back and said coaxingly, 'I'll do without the sausages if the idea really offends you.' He was holding her against his chest so that she could feel the mat of hairs which covered it. They were smooth and very black, almost like fur, and shorter ones darkened his forearms and the backs of his long fingers. She looked down at his hands, loosely clasped round her, comparing the colour with her winter-pale skin. They tightened briefly as he followed her gaze, and he mumured seductively into her ear, 'You cook my breakfast, and while you're doing it, I'll make your coffee and toast. Then I'll get lunch.' He paused for a moment. 'And then I'll make love to you. And tonight I'll take you out to dinner and when we get back I'll make love to you again.'

She chuckled and turned her head until she could look into his face. Loading her voice with scepticism, she asked, 'Promises or ambition?' and he grinned and bit her ear, then rested his chin on her shoulder.

'You'll have to wait and see.'

Taking him by surprise she wriggled free, and from the safety of the bathroom door, scoffed, 'Don't you mean that *you* will?'

He was in the kitchen when she came out from her shower, walking round with a piece of toast in his hand as he plugged in the percolator and assembled mugs and glasses on the worktop. He bit into it as she watched, but any hope that he might find it sufficient was dashed when he fetched the bacon and eggs and everything else out of the fridge and arrayed them in a line along the table.

Feebly, she protested, 'I don't know how anyone can seriously contemplate eating all that at half-past seven in the morning. It's nauseating. You surely don't have it every day?'

'Ah, but I do,' he affirmed. 'Going off marriage already?'

Single mindedly, she said, 'Then who normally cooks it?'

'I do.' She opened her mouth indignantly and he put the last of his toast into her mouth, silencing her, and added, 'But I don't like cooking.'

Swallowing the toast, she demanded, 'You mean I was lured into marriage for this?'

'The only alternative was a service flat and I didn't want to move.'

'Great,' she muttered, sliding a frying pan on to the cooker. 'Now I know my true worth.' She surveyed the row of dials helplessly for a moment. 'All right—how do you switch this thing on? It looks as though you need a driving licence for it.'

He leaned over and turned a couple of the dials, and with an expression of distaste she broke two eggs into the non-stick pan. 'Wait until I tell everyone how I spent the first morning of my honeymoon!'

She had her back to him but she heard him laugh before he slid his hands under her sweater and reached round to cradle her breasts. 'Would you really do that? And I thought women were usually more delicate.'

She had laid herself wide open to that. She grinned, then squirmed away from him, uneasily aware that the effects of his practised touch must soon be apparent to him. Half-serious, she said tartly, 'Stop that unless you want your breakfast burned.'

For a second his fingers continued to flex pleasurably,

then he stepped back. 'And wait until I tell everyone how my advances were spurned by my bride of less than a day.'

'That's a statement that is open to several different interpretations.' She sent him a sideways glance and tentatively turned the knob for what she hoped was the grill. 'Some of them might reflect unfavourably on your prowess.'

'What puny little claws,' he jeered. 'And you've just switched the oven on. Were you going to roast the bacon?' He put her to one side and capably assembled everything under the grill, saying, 'Now watch,' as he adjusted the various dials to the required heat.

She noted the controls carefully, but she wasn't going to let him see, so she asked irrelevantly, 'What time do the papers come?'

'They should be here now. Earn your keep and go and fetch them.'

She pulled a face at him and went into the hall, ridiculously pleased at the thought that she would be doing this every day. Her eyes on the headlines, she dawdled back and found he had put the bread in the toaster for her and their orange juice was already poured and on the table.

His competence made her feel superfluous, and after she had fetched the percolator she sat pretending to read the paper, but in reality watching him over the top. How tall was he? she wondered. Five or six inches over her own five feet nine, the minimum height for a model. His back was broad under the dark grey of his casual shirt, and memory suddenly presented her with a picture of him naked, powerful muscles moving under the supple skin. Abruptly her blood raced, and she lowered her eyes to the paper in earnest until he slid a plate of toast in front of her and said, 'Don't expect this every morning. I'm a dedicated chauvinist at heart.'

They read the papers while they ate, then did the crosswords together, or at least she watched while he wrote the answers in, proffering solutions which he mostly rejected.

To one of her suggestions, he scorned, 'Good God, woman, you're practically illiterate!' and she pointed out huffily that as a writer he could be expected to know more words than she did, afterwards displaying excessive triumph when she answered a clue he hadn't been able to.

They finished eating and cleared up, then went into the lounge and he put some tapes on and showed an equal contempt for her musical knowledge. His collection was entirely classical, and it was immediately obvious to him that she couldn't tell Mozart from Mendelssohn. In retaliation, she proved to him that he was completely ignorant when it came to the modern music scene and taunted him with being old, so that he pulled her down on to the wide settee, muttering threateningly, 'I'll show you who's old!'

Between laughter and a wild excitement, she fought him for every item of her clothes and slipped away when he slackened his grip on her, fleeing for the door. He brought her down almost at once so that they ended up together on the rug in front of the fire, breathless from their struggles, hearts thudding with exertion and desire.

It needed no more than the meeting of their mouths to catapult them both to the edge of control, and she was jubilant when he moved swiftly to take possession of her because she knew that this time he was the one unable to delay, the speed and intensity of their mutual rise of passion catching him unprepared. When he subsided against her, his breath coming rapidly, she smiled with a contentment that was mental as well as physical, and murmured, 'I thought that was scheduled for after lunch.'

His body shook with laughter. 'Yes—well, this afternoon's item on the agenda may possibly have to be postponed for a little while.' They lay for a moment longer, the firelight playing on them, then he began to draw away. She refused to release her hold on him, and he laughed huskily in his throat and said, 'I know this is going to sound terribly unromantic, but the truth is that I'm burning, so let go!'

She obeyed and he rolled away from her and sat up, rubbing down his shoulder and arm. 'God, that was getting hot!' He looked down to where she still lay, his eyes narrowing in the brilliant smile that turned her heart over. 'Married under twenty-four hours, and already I'm exhausted, bruised and burnt!'

'All of life is a risk.'

He sneered. 'You have the nerve to offer me platitudes for comfort?'

'All right.' She raised herself up beside him and he curved an arm round her. 'I'll get the lunch instead. How about that?'

He kissed her, his hand straying reflectively up her thigh. 'That's more like it. I thought for a while you weren't going to offer.'

She selected a packet of moussaka from the deep freeze, and while she was checking through the drawers, discovered the instructions for the cooker so that she was able to heat it without assistance. The deep freeze was well stocked, and at least she didn't have to worry about what sort of food to give him. He wouldn't have bought it for himself if he didn't like it. They had ice-cream with black cherries afterwards, and Grant observed, 'I can see you're a superb cook, providing everything is frozen or tinned.'

'More or less,' Fran admitted. She was curled up in the corner of the settee, heavy eyed and yawning from the effects of two large glasses of wine. She didn't even realise she had slept until she felt Grant shaking her shoulder and opened her eyes to the mug of coffee he was holding in front of her.

'Here,' he said. 'I thought I'd better not leave you any longer. You've been asleep for nearly two hours.'

She yawned again. 'I could sleep for a week. It's the after effects of being disturbed in the night and then woken again at six.'

He laughed. 'So you do remember.' When she looked down evasively, he added, 'But you shouldn't be tired. You were in bed by half-past four after all.'

'Yes,' she retorted. 'And not even taken out to dinner. Some honeymoon this is turning out to be.'

In the end they didn't go out that night either. Grant had checked the answer-phone while she slept and discovered that the studio wanted some re-writing on the script of his play. He didn't intend starting it for several days, but he wanted to watch the video recording of one of his previous television plays to clear up some point in his mind. Fran had only ever seen the theatre production of his first one, and she was fascinated, feeling a glow of pride when his name came up on the screen. Grant watched it with critical coolness, and when the tape ended, he commented, 'Well, at least one can learn from one's mistakes. Not one of my best efforts, though the director was nominated for an award. Let's hope he wins—he deserves it.'

He got up and switched the recorder off, then smiled down at her and said softly, 'Bed, Mrs Mercier, and prepare to eat your words.'

To Fran, the days and weeks that followed were pure happiness. They disagreed over some things—he continued to tell her that her taste in music was execrable and refused to have Radio One on at breakfast time, so she played it while he was working in his study, and in retaliation she complained of the volume at which he played Tannhauser, and drew the line at the Brandenburg Concertos.

They went out quite a lot in the evenings, but when he began to work regularly again during the day she found she was restless, and told him she wanted to take over from the contract cleaners he'd always had in to do the flat.

With faint caution, he said, 'Are you sure?' and Fran knew he was remembering the state of Sacha's flat the first time he had seen it.

'It's all right,' she told him. 'That was Sacha's natural environment, not mine.'

In fact they were well matched over what they considered comfortable. Grant was obsessively ordered in his study, refusing to allow her to touch anything, but otherwise they were neither particularly tidy nor untidy. She was scrupulous in the kitchen and the bathrooms, and cleaned everywhere else before it could begin to offend her—an arrangement which seemed to suit Grant equally well. In the first few days they got a washing machine and tumble dryer, and the following week, to her deep delight, he took her out and bought her a car.

Her delight turned to terror however, when it came to the point of actually driving it. It was nearly three years since she had passed her test and she had never been behind the wheel of a car since. She almost needed to learn from the beginning again, and Grant drove her into the suburbs every day, then made her take over and patiently tutored her until he considered she was safe to be let loose in the city traffic on her own. She wondered how he had the courage to sit calmly beside her the first time she took it down Regent Street, but when she told him so he only grinned and said, 'If you want the truth I'm bloody terrified! Now watch the pedestrians—otherwise you're doing all right.'

He also provided her with an assortment of credit cards and gave her *carte blanche* to get what she considered necessary in the line of clothes. Invitations had come in for various dinners and functions they would be going to, and he had been mildly surprised by her meagre wardrobe.

He moved her few dresses from side to side with his hand and said, 'I thought models had a vast collection of clothes for the gay lives they lead.'

His brows were raised in enquiry, and she gave a small shrug. 'I did have quite a few, but they weren't the sort of things you would like. I gave them away and I wouldn't get any more until I knew what I would be needing.'

It was the only reference he ever made to her former career. By tacit consent they avoided discussion of anything in their past which might cause friction. Once Grant caught himself up and she knew he had been about to mention Julia, and on another occasion she said something about Seth, and meeting his suddenly cool stare, became aware that by the way she spoke and the warmth in her tone she had revealed some element of affection for the younger man. With a slight shock she realised he thought Seth had been her lover, and thinking back it came to her that she had never actually denied it—only that they had been living together. Perhaps she should have made it plain then that they had never been more than friends, but the basic injustice of Grant's attitude annoyed her. Defiantly, she said, 'There's no need for you to look at me like that. He's married himself now.'

There was a pause before Grant commented sardonically, 'He transfers his affections quickly.'

She had seldom heard that note in his voice before

and wished heartily that she had never mentioned Seth. The information that it was a shotgun wedding would hardly add to Grant's opinion of him either, so she shrugged and turned away, and it was Grant who changed the subject.

It was the nearest they ever got to a serious difference until the time he queried her spending. He had been generous in everything since their marriage, taking pleasure in giving her jewellery and other things she had never dreamed of owning, and when he first mentioned the cost of her clothes she was more than ready to agree with him that she had gone over the top.

It wasn't so much that she wanted them for herself as the fact that she felt insecure when she was out with him, afraid of letting him down by some unwitting social blunder, and over-conscious of the trace of border counties accent which still sometimes showed in her speech. She wanted him to be proud of her, and to appear beautiful and well dressed—to see other men's eyes follow her and know they envied him—gave her confidence.

Because of it she had bought without thinking enough of the cost, and there had also been some expensive mistakes in the beginning before she discovered he was curiously puritanical about bared flesh in public where she was concerned. In private it was different, and the beautiful nightdresses she had purchased before the wedding were practically unworn. He had told her with amusement to put them with his pyjamas and keep them for when they stayed in hotels.

When he told her the total of what she had spent she was shattered. She stared at him, bereft of speech, and he smiled faintly. 'It's all right, we're not broke and I can stand it, but give me a bit of warning for any very expensive item in the future.'

Almost in tears, she gathered her breath for a

passionate apology. He was folding away the bank statement with its accusing DR against the final figure, and seeing her eyes on it he said non-committally, 'Don't worry, all that isn't yours. I've bought some shares, and I've spent quite a lot recently on new equipment for the farm. It's just that I like to have a rough idea of what the situation is. I have a standing order so I need to keep enough in the current account to cover it.'

It was said with the intention of letting her down lightly she knew, but suddenly she realised what the standing order must be for, and her remorse was smothered, replaced by a wave of hate. Flippantly, she said, 'I'm sorry. I'd forgotten you had two wives to keep.'

She knew the acid had shown through her tone, and he raised his eyes quickly before she had time to clear the mutinous expression from her face. He continued his regard for a moment, then said evenly, 'It isn't anything you need to think about.'

His voice was too controlled to be natural, and turning away from her he began to open the rest of his post. She wanted to apologise for her extravagance, and tell him as well that she was sorry for that tart, flippant reply, but before she could frame the words he swore abruptly at something he had been reading and reached for the phone, a heavy frown tightening his face.

From his conversation it was obvious he was enraged. She melted away to give him time to calm down, and afterwards she couldn't summon sufficient courage to reintroduce the subject, quietening her conscience with the resolve to never again give him cause to mention her expenditure.

The incident left her uneasy, but otherwise she viewed life with eager anticipation. Grant laughed at her, mocked her areas of ignorance, and got her to admit when he found her singing to it that she was starting to enjoy some of his music. Sometimes she caught him looking at her with a waiting, watching air, as though he had expected her to do something or say something which she hadn't, but he gave no sign that he regretted their precipitate marriage.

Her fears and doubts gradually faded away, and she even began to view their eventual return to the country with only mild apprehension. It might be pleasant to spend the summer there—perhaps to ride again, and pick up old friendships. Perhaps to bear Grant's child.

The thought occurred to her so often that she wondered ruefully if she was getting broody. The passion he showed her was still as undiminished as her own response. Sometimes he only looked at her with that slight, narrowed smile, and she was on fire for him.

He knew it, and plagued her when they were out, stripping her with his eyes in company, and smiling at her betraying flush. When she objected he told her there was something exquisitely erotic about picturing her naked in the middle of some respectable gathering, each of them knowing what the other was thinking but unable to do anything about their desires until the evening was ended. And she looked forward to that ending as ardently as he did, Fran admitted. She had come a long way since her wedding night. Grant had taught her all the refinements of lovemaking, and no man ever had a more willing pupil.

He never told her he loved her, but she managed to convince herself that the omission was unimportant. Except for that she was utterly happy—so utterly incredibly happy that she would wake in the night afraid, lost in a nameless terror that he had been given to her in mistake and he would be taken from her again, because it was too much happiness to be granted to one person, and it was never intended that she should know the continuing joy of being with him and loving him.

Sometimes she disturbed him when she pressed her cheek against his back, desperate to reassure herself that he was real and alive. When his breathing grew even again she would whisper how she loved him and how much he meant to her, half-hoping that her words might penetrate his sleep and one night he would tell her of his own love in return.

CHAPTER SIX

THE blow, when it came, caught her completely unawares. They had gone to the dinner where the television awards were being presented, and Fran was wearing a new dress which Grant had chosen for her himself, paying an exorbitant price for it as though to cancel out the scene where he had called her to book for her spending.

She was more assured on these occasions now. Though she seldom enjoyed them she managed to give the appearance of it, smiling and sparkling when it was necessary, radiating enjoyment to the people who mattered. She was prepared to do anything that might help Grant, and vigorously denied, when he asked her, that she found them boring.

When the meal was over and they gave the awards, she clapped dutifully, then with more enthusiasm for the director of Grant's play when he won. At least this was interesting for Grant. A lot of the people he knew and worked with, and he was quietly getting the feel of the evening, picking up the subtle nuances which were present in a gathering of professionals like these, and which might provide him with useful information in the future about who were the up-and-coming men as well as the present geniuses.

They would have to linger at the bar when it was over so that he could go on garnering information and gossip, and she sighed inwardly and wondered if she dared slip her feet out of her shoes for a few moments in preparation. These evenings were all so much alike that they blurred into one in her mind. The men would

greet each other as though they hadn't met for years,
then Grant would introduce her and she would stand
holding her drink and appearing interested while they
talked about things which were totally beyond her
understanding. She would tell herself that it was her job
and no more boring than the tedious hours she used to
spend in front of the camera, and eventually they would
escape and go home.

This one followed the familiar pattern. The women
all kissed each other with cries of, 'Darling!' and she
wondered how soon she would be well enough known
to get similar treatment. She was startled when a
middle-aged woman, completely strange to her,
suddenly broke off a conversation with someone else
and hurried towards her, arms outstretched. It was
obvious to Fran that she was about to be kissed, and
she sent Grant a swift glance, puzzled and enquiring.

He was standing frozen, staring at the woman. As she
drew nearer he moved quickly as though to intervene,
but it was too late. Fran found both her hands seized,
was kissed on each cheek, then her hand was joined
with Grant's and the woman peered up at them both,
beaming with delight.

'My darlings!' she exclaimed. 'You're together again!
Oh, I always knew it would happen—didn't I say so? It
was so plain that you were meant for each other that I
knew that silly separation could never last!'

She took a few steps back towards her friends,
beckoning them, and Fran heard Grant swearing
viciously under his breath. She was too stunned herself
to do anything about correcting the misapprehension,
and anyway she wouldn't have known what to say.

It had all happened so quickly, in a matter of
seconds, that she was unable to formulate any thought,
or question what Grant's reaction must be, apart from
his barely hidden fury.

She heard him mutter savagely, 'Why can't the stupid bloody cow wear her glasses, for God's sake!' then he went after her, calling out, 'Brenda!' in a vain attempt to silence her.

Inevitably by now they were attracting attention. Grant lowered his voice as he said, 'Brenda, this isn't Julia,' but several people overheard and turned curious heads towards them. Fran stood still, feeling sick, watching and listening to Grant's explanations. Was she meant to go on smiling, even at a moment like this?

Brenda looked confused then distressed, and turned back to look at her, making helpless little gestures. 'I must apologise ... but they are so alike...' With lagging steps she returned and took Fran's hand, pressing it awkwardly as she gazed into her face, short-sighted and earnest. 'My dear, I'm so sorry ... so embarrassing for both of us, but really I was so certain ...'

Fran found she really was still smiling. She said, 'It's perfectly all right—don't worry about it,' aware of the whispering starting up round them. Grant reappeared at her side and muttered, 'Careful, we've got a photographer!' and Brenda made her escape, still shaking her head in confusion.

He watched her go, rage dangerously near the surface, and nervously and placatingly, Fran said, 'Grant, you can't really blame her if she hasn't seen Julia for some time.'

'She hasn't seen her for three bloody years, but even without her glasses she should be able to see that you're at least four inches taller, apart from anything else!'

'Well, I admit it was a bit embarrassing, but let's forget it. It's over now, and ...'

Tersely, he interrupted, 'Oh, no it isn't! It's only just begun! Smile!'

She did as he ordered, just in time for a barrage of

exploding flash bulbs, as the reporters, scenting news, deserted the stars of the evening they had been sent to cover. Grant said, 'Don't answer any of them!' and she kept her smile fixed as he tried to extricate them, parrying the questions shooting at them from all sides.

'Is the lady your wife, Mr Mercier? How long have you been married? Where did you meet? How long since your divorce? Where is your first wife now, Mr Mercier?'

They went on unceasingly. Fran felt buffeted, astounded by the impertinence of the questions, and terrified that Grant would lose his tenuous control over his temper and antagonise them. At the moment he sounded deceptively tolerant, laughing, and only raising his voice in order to make himself heard, though underneath she knew he was boiling. But he was also used to dealing with the press, and after a while they dispersed, not entirely satisfied, but anxious to get the stories in to their editors.

Grant let out a harsh sigh, and said, 'We shall have to wait until tomorrow to see what they make of it,' then turned towards the exit. 'Let's get out of here while we've got the chance.'

The phone was ringing when they got home. Grant picked it up and replaced it, then switched over to the answer-phone which for some reason he had forgotten to do before he went out. He made no comment on the earlier events, but he was still awake, one arm behind his head, when Fran at last went off to sleep.

When the newspapers came the next day she read them with stunned disbelief. She had been upset at the time of the incident, but not as deeply disturbed as Grant because she couldn't honestly see how it could be of enough interest to the public to cause any great stir. Reading what appeared, she realised that what interest was lacking in the facts would be made up for in innuendo. They made it riveting.

There were two photographs, the first of Grant and
Julia, taken, she guessed, in the same theatre foyer
where she had seen them all those years ago, then
beside it, one taken last night. For a moment she even
had trouble distinguishing them herself—Grant in
evening dress, herself and Julia in similar black dresses,
blonde hair drawn away from their faces and smoothly
pinned up at the back. It carried the caption, 'Which is
the current Mrs Mercier?' and went on for several
paragraphs of carefully worded speculation.

Disgusted, she pushed the paper away and reached
for another, aware as she did so of Grant's bleak gaze
fixed on her. As soon as she saw it she knew why.

It was on the gossip page this time. Two photographs
the same as before, drawing attention to the likeness,
then another one of Grant and Julia in a restaurant,
smiling at each other. Even before Fran's eyes went to
the words printed underneath she knew somehow that it
was recent.

It began, 'An intriguing situation has been drawn to
our attention . . .' and Fran thought dully that it had
been brought to hers as well. 'Grant Mercier, well-
known television personality and playwright, married in
January to the astonishingly lookalike Mrs Mercier
number two, is here pictured two weeks later dining in
a restaurant with Mrs Mercier number one.' The
columnist wondered what could be in the wind.

He wasn't the only one, Fran thought, stricken.
Carefully controlling her voice, she said, 'This was
taken after we were married.'

'Yes,' he admitted. 'I suppose I should have told you
I was meeting her, but at the time it just seemed simpler
not to. I didn't know that had been taken. There was
some sort of celebration going on a few tables away and
there were flashes going off everywhere.'

Stonily, she said, 'So you thought I'd never find out.'

'There *is* nothing to find out. Look, I'll tell you now what I should obviously have told you before. I rang Julia to tell her we were married . . .'

'How civilised,' Fran interrupted acidly.

'Damn it, Fran, will you *listen*! I knew there was always the possibility of last night's development and I simply wanted to warn her so that she would be prepared for it. She's probably got reporters all round her front door by now, and after what happened to us you must surely realise that it's too easy to let them rattle you into giving a wrong answer if the whole thing is sprung on you without warning.'

'She could have said, "No comment",' Fran observed coldly. 'She could easily have known nothing about our marriage. As a matter of fact, I would have thought it was better if she didn't. She could have told them so with perfect truth, and that would have been a protection in itself.'

'And the questions that come after that? How do you feel now you do know about it, Mrs Mercier? Do you think there is any significance in the fact that your ex-husband's new wife bears such a close resemblance to you? Would you like to give us your comments, Mrs Mercier?' He drew a deep breath and looked across at her. 'Have a heart, Fran.'

She lowered her eyes to the photograph again, the sickness of the initial shock fading as she realised she believed him. Ironically, because she trusted Julia. Knowing he had married again, she would never have agreed to meet him except for a very good reason. Fran knew she had absolutely nothing to fear from her in the sense of physical infidelity, but it wasn't physical infidelity she was afraid of. Unfaithfulness in the mind had as much power to destroy and could rouse just as much jealousy, and it was against Grant's thoughts and emotions that she had no defence.

His insistence on secrecy for their wedding now appeared in a new light. At the time there had been no reason to believe it was anything but what he said—that he didn't want their privacy invaded—but then she hadn't fully grasped that whatever he did was new, nor had it occurred to her that the likeness between Julia and herself was something the press would leap on. If the photographer outside the register office had been more alert and recognised Grant the situation would have blown up then, catching Julia unprepared.

Indicating the picture in the restaurant, she said, 'This was after we were married. Why didn't you tell her before?'

'I tried to but she was away. I couldn't get hold of her.'

'So that's why you wanted to keep our wedding quiet,' she said, her voice flat. 'To protect Julia.'

He hesitated. 'Not only Julia. Both of you.'

'I don't remember you giving me any warning of what to expect,' she commented sharply.

'There was no need. I was ready to deal with it, and it was pointless to worry you with something which might never happen.'

'All right,' she said at last. 'I'll accept that you wanted to save her from unpleasantness since it's hardly her fault, but a phone call would have done it. It didn't need a candlelit dinner for two.'

Beginning to show impatience, he said forcefully, 'It was seven-thirty in a packed restaurant with a party going on ten yards away! Hardly the setting for a night of nostalgia! It so happened that when I rang her she was coming up to London the following day, so I said I'd meet her after I'd finished at the studio. We had a meal while we discussed it and afterwards I put her in a taxi back to her hotel.'

'Without even a good night kiss?' Fran enquired cynically.

It struck home and Grant closed his eyes wearily. 'We *were* married for six years.'

Fran stared at him in disbelief. His tone wasn't even defensive—he had spoken without the slightest trace of guilt, and stunned, she realised he felt none. It seemed that his guilt, his concern, was reserved for Julia. She wanted to rage and scream at him, and vent her helpless jealousy with her fists, but she daren't, and it would accomplish nothing anyway. In a hard voice she said, 'It all sounds terribly friendly and considerate. Perhaps she regrets now that she divorced you. After all, she hasn't re-married.'

'Oh, for God's sake!' he exclaimed. He slapped his open palm down on the paper in front of him. 'Look, you've seen this rubbish. This is what they can do with a simple likeness on a day when they're short of news, but that's all it is—rubbish. They're not actually saying anything, just inviting the readers to let their imagination run riot and see if it suggests anything scandalous to them. Everyone will watch us for a while just in case there *is* a bit of scandal somewhere, and no doubt the press will hang round hopefully, but then it will die down. We've all been annoyed but nobody's harmed. I've been waiting for it and I had my answers ready, but I had to be certain Julia had as well. You said yourself that it wasn't her fault this had arisen, and the very least I can do is to try to make sure it doesn't rebound on her as well.'

Fran's lips were dry and she moistened them. 'Possibly I'm dense but I can't think of any questions which could be so very terrible.'

He said deliberately, 'Can't you? Then try these for size. Have you ever met your ex-husband's second wife, Mrs Mercier? Can you tell us where he met her?' He paused, then went on, 'See what your imagination could make of the answers to those if you were a reporter digging for dirt.'

Her eyes flew to his face. 'But . . . but there's nothing for them to find.'

'Prove it!' he challenged. He shoved the newspapers away from him with a gesture of distaste. 'Look what they managed to come up with there. Oh, it would all be very carefully phrased—nothing we could sue them for, but unfortunately I offended one or two members of the press in my early days and they wouldn't lose a chance to come back at me.'

Fran was silent. It was a short step from gossip column to gutter press, and they could suggest something salacious merely by virtuously denying that they *were* suggesting it. If they discovered she once lived within sight of Grant and Julia the implications were obvious, but a heavily veiled insinuation that his marriage had foundered because of a torrid affair with a teenager would only be damaging to them, and it was Julia he was mostly concerned for.

Grant was slowly pacing the kitchen, his hands shoved into the pockets of his bathrobe. He went to the window and let up the blind, then swore and pulled it down again. 'I'd better go and get dressed. There's a couple of them outside and they won't go away until I've spoken to them.'

She nodded, then said as he reached the door, 'I still don't see how Julia could really be affected by any of this. We're the ones who won't come out of it smelling of roses if they try to make out we were having an affair, and anyway she knows there is no foundation for it. I only ever saw you in the distance after you were married—I never so much as spoke to you, so I don't see why she should be particularly upset.'

Even to her own ears her voice sounded pettish, and Grant halted and half-turned back towards her. 'Don't be uncharitable, Fran. She's not as tough as you, and she would be both embarrassed and humiliated by that sort of publicity. I'm not exactly overjoyed at the prospect of my role in it either.'

'And I suppose it isn't reasonable for me to feel humiliated,' Fran retorted bitterly. 'I've no right to be resentful if everyone now regards me as a sort of ... clone of your first wife! I might have taken comfort from the fact that at least I was the one left in possession, but after that photograph there would seem to be some doubt about it!'

'I'm sorry about that. It's unfortunate that we were seen together.'

Incredulously, Fran noted that he was apologising not for the fact that he had taken Julia there, but that it had been made public. Sudden, violent anger seized her. It must have shown in her face, and his expression arrested, Grant said, 'For God's sake, Fran, you're not jealous! You must surely know you've no cause to be!'

Of course she knew. There had been three years when Julia might have taken him back but she hadn't, and even if she'd had thoughts of it, her principles were too high to allow her to consider it now. But the jealousy was still there, and to hide it she said acidly, 'Other people are bound to think I have reason to be. I might be tougher than Julia, but I shall still find all the speculation about us unpleasant.'

'I've said I'm sorry for that and I am, and yes, with hindsight it would have been very much better if it had all been done on the phone. At the time I'm afraid I was only concerned with getting together so that we should tell the same story. As far as the press are concerned, you and I met at that party where you collapsed. We don't want them delving any further.'

'I expect you're right,' she agreed woodenly. 'Though anyone in the valley could tell them there was nothing of interest.'

'It wouldn't be wise to rely on it.'

She looked up, startled, and he held her eyes with a level gaze and said, 'Not if they went back far enough.' He paused again, and she felt her face wash with scarlet colour under his steady regard. 'There's always talk in a village, Fran—you know that. For our sake as well it's best not stirred up again.'

She was speechless, her face and neck still burning from the tide of heat. He gave a small shrug, then to her inexpressible relief there was a long, insistent peal on the doorbell. He said irritably, 'Oh hell, ignore it. I'll be down to them in a minute,' and she was left staring after him, her mind grappling with the inferences of his oblique statement.

She felt sick with shame as she considered them. She had known he left home to escape her, but it had never even crossed her mind that her pursuit of him might have been noticed by others and he was escaping from the gossip she had caused as well.

She would never dare mention his meeting with Julia again and she wished she had never learned of it. Gazing into her half-empty coffee cup, she tried to banish her miserable, suspicious thoughts, but she found herself wondering if Grant had always kept in touch with Julia; if there had been other times, since their marriage, when he had met her and there hadn't been a photographer on the scene.

In her heart she knew there hadn't, but she was shocked, her confidence shattered. Grant had known last night what to expect, but his fury over Brenda's mistake had not been because of its effects on her, but on Julia. She had come second. The knowledge resurrected all her doubts. She was back to the beginning again, unsure of herself and of him, and against her will her eyes were drawn again to the picture taken in the restaurant.

What did Julia possess that evoked such staunch love

and **loyalty**? And why, oh why, did the camera have to capture so exactly that softened expression in Grant's eyes as he smiled at her?

When he came back in she was still sitting in the same position at the table. He glanced at her, his dark brows drawn heavily together, and said, 'I'm beginning to think it might be a good idea to go home straight away. I want to get down to some uninterrupted writing anyway, and we should be free of this nuisance.'

He had been thinking of it for some time, and she had been quite agreeable when he mentioned it before. Now, however, the prospect filled her with dread. She exclaimed quickly, 'Oh no!' then tried to moderate her reaction as she saw his surprise. 'I mean, wouldn't it look as though we were running away? That we really had got something to hide?'

'Frankly, I don't give a damn how it looks.' He paused, watching her. 'Don't you want to go?'

'Of course I do,' she returned, forcing a smile. 'But I don't want anyone to think we're turning tail, and it would seem odd when we've accepted for several parties and dinners. And aren't you supposed to be declaring something open?'

'I could come back for it. Would you mind missing the parties?'

They reminded her all too strongly of the interminable affairs she used to attend with Seth and it would be a relief to miss them, but she said lightly, 'I was rather looking forward to them actually. I must have somewhere to show off my new necklace and earrings, and besides, I haven't had time yet to get used to being married to Grant Mercier, the sought-after playwright. I get quite a lot of reflected glory, you know—everyone is terribly nice to me.'

Even without Grant's quick frown she knew it was the wrong thing to have said. He was quietly scornful of the hostesses who regarded his presence merely as a social achievement. He would spend hours talking over problems and techniques with fellow writers and those in the television business, but it made him uncomfortable to be paraded and lionised.

He said, 'All right, we'll forget it for a while, but don't accept any more invitations.' His voice was unrevealing, but Fran suspected he was disappointed in her, and confirming it, he said, 'Life can't be all play, Fran—I do have to work as well, and though I have a good manager in charge of the farm, there are still things I need to discuss and oversee.'

He went out, and she sat for a moment longer. The whole issue had started out with a near-row over Grant seeing Julia without her knowledge, and despairingly she wondered how it could possibly have ended with her being the one in the wrong.

There was a constraint between them for the next few days, though she couldn't honestly say it was due entirely to Grant. He had been remote occasionally before when his mind was heavily involved with thoughts of the play he was on, and it might have been the reason this time. They went out a couple of times in the evening, once to one of the parties, and unexpectedly she enjoyed it since she met a girl she liked and had lost touch with. They had started out in modelling together, but Margot had progressed through television commercials to acting parts, and was now quite successful.

Fran gaily introduced her to Grant, and was inwardly gratified when she looked him over with open envy, and said, 'I'd swap my career for him any day.'

'Oh, being married to a writer isn't nearly as glamorous as you might think,' Grant drawled. 'People are inclined to get the wrong idea about us, particularly if we write for television. They think we spend all our time mingling with the rich and the famous, but actually we can be very silent and boring, can't we Fran?'

'Sometimes,' she agreed uncertainly. 'Though it's not as bad as you're making it sound.'

'But it's not the exciting life that outsiders might imagine,' he insisted.

She looked across at him, and meeting his mocking smile, realised with a sense of shock that he was slightly drunk. Uncomfortably, she said, 'Perhaps not. It all depends on what you consider exciting. A lot of people wouldn't find that kind of life enjoyable anyway.'

She was embarrassed and beginning to feel apprehensive. She had never known Grant to drink too much before and she didn't know how to handle him. Observing her unease he smiled at her again, then turned to the other girl and said, 'So don't swap your career until you're certain what you'll be getting in exchange. Ask my wife.'

The sparring little episode ruined the rest of the evening for Fran, and she was thankful when they left. They were silent in the taxi on the way home, but inside the apartment he put his arm round her and she shook him off irritably.

'Stop it—you're drunk.'

His hand fell away from her at once. Agreeably he said, 'Who should know that better than I? Another fascinating aspect of my character which you haven't been privileged to observe before. And I'm not so very drunk, my darling, or I shouldn't have been able to say that. Note also that I am quite docile. I'm not one of your noisy, aggressive drunks—quite the reverse, in fact. It is merely that under the influence I perhaps have a tendency to say things which prudence would normally forbid.'

'Like that rubbish you were talking to Margot.' She

glared at him in exasperation. 'What was behind all that, for heaven's sake?'

'Merely a little friendly advice—what else?'

'You made it sound as though I married you for the life I expected to lead!'

'The mingling with the rich and the famous? But don't you enjoy it, darling? You always assured me you did when I asked you, and you've never even hinted that you didn't want to go to any of those bloody affairs. I've watched you getting ready for them, preparing to outshine all the other dresses and furs that would be there. Not that I'm complaining—you look quite delightful in furs, and it's a small price to pay for your contentment.'

Fran bit her lip, then said in a stifled voice, 'Actually I don't enjoy them, but I thought you more or less had to go to them so I was making the best of it. If you want the truth, I'm usually bored a lot of the time.'

'Ah, the truth,' he said consideringly. 'Which is it, I wonder? What you told me before, or what you're saying now? Because if it's what you're saying now, then you certainly had me fooled! You positively lit up at some of those dinner parties, darling, and if a man happened to be a millionaire you were dazzling.'

'Because you need millionaires as backers for your plays and you never know when it might pay dividends! Would you rather I was rude?'

He raised his brows. 'You mean it was all for my benefit?'

'Yes,' she muttered. 'Though I don't suppose you'll believe it.'

'You suppose quite rightly. I wanted to go home, if you remember, but no. There were a few functions where I had to be exhibited first, and you had to display your jewellery. You're surely not claiming that was for my benefit as well!'

She looked at him with a sense of helplessness and found he was watching her cynically, his eyes still alert and intelligent, despite the alcohol.

'Well?' he challenged.

'No,' she said after a pause. 'I'm not claiming it in that instance, but it wasn't because of the invitations that I didn't want to go.'

The glance he sent her was rich with scepticism. 'Really, darling? Then enlighten me—what *was* the reason?'

Shrugging, she turned away from him. 'Nothing that matters now.'

'Of all the answers to a question that is possibly the most irritating,' he observed dispassionately. He walked over to the sideboard and took out the Scotch bottle and a glass, swinging round to face her again with the drink in his hand. Her lips tightened, and he said, 'If you're about to point out that I've already had enough, I know I have, darling, but I feel like having a little more, so go to bed and don't bother me. Save your wifely concern for the hangover I shall have in the morning.'

Fran didn't see him again until breakfast time. She knew he must have slept on the settee, but he was showered and changed when he appeared, and if he was suffering he gave no sign of it. His manner was so normal that she wondered how much of the previous evening he remembered. But he wouldn't have forgotten, she knew—his brain had still been keen enough. He was indicating to her that he wanted the subject ignored, and on the whole she was relieved. She might be smarting at the injustice of what he believed of her, but explanations could make things worse and it was better left.

Sacha rang towards evening, breaking a long silence. Fran knew she had landed a job in Rome and gone off triumphantly to model some new young designer's spring collection, but that had been weeks ago, and when she heard her voice, Fran said drily, 'It must have been some assignment.'

Sacha gurgled on the other end of the line. 'Darling, I met this delightful Italian and decided to have a little holiday afterwards. There's a bit of post for you here, by the way, so why don't you come round and collect it and we'll have some girl talk.'

Grant was working in his study and she had put a cold meal ready, so she said, 'Half an hour?'

'Fine, sweetie. I'll tell you *all* about *everything*!'

Fran was still grinning when she went in to tell Grant where she was going, and he looked up and commented, 'That's a very anticipatory smile.'

'Sacha's back,' she explained. 'I'm just going round to hear all about the delights of Rome in the spring and one Italian in particular.'

'Take a taxi then. It's difficult to park round there, and I can pick you up when you're ready.'

'There's no need for you to come out for me,' she protested.

'It's no trouble. Just give me a ring when you want fetching.' He watched her for a moment longer, his expression enigmatic, then added, 'Enjoy yourself.'

She said, 'I will,' and went out feeling a little deflated, and wondering if she had imagined that he didn't want her to go. Perhaps he thought seeing Sacha would reawaken a yearning for her old life, she thought with a spurt of acid resentment. Strangely, he was sensitive about the difference in their ages, but while it was true that she was now mixing in an older age group than she had been used to, it didn't bother her and there was nothing in the past she wanted to go back to.

Sacha greeted her with enthusiasm. 'A drink, darling, then we talk,' she declared, and Fran agreed since she wasn't driving, absently picking up her letters as she went by and stuffing them into her bag. The flat was more chaotic than ever, she noticed. She must have had a leavening influence when she lived there.

Sacha was already seated cross-legged on a huge new floor cushion in the most garish shade of purple Fran had ever seen. She said, 'Your turn first, darling. How's married life and that tall, handsome, virile husband of yours?'

Fran shrugged and smiled. 'He's tall, handsome and virile, and married life is wonderful. Let's hear about your Italian.'

'My dear, you should have seen him,' Sacha returned, shuddering ecstatically. 'He had the most beautiful liquid brown eyes I have ever seen and he stripped off like a Roman god. He was mad to make me his countess, or whatever it is in Italy. Isn't that too marvellously flattering?'

Fran agreed, prompting her into further lyrical descriptions, and when Sacha finally ran dry, she enquired, 'So what was the hitch?'

'The usual one, darling—he'd hardly got a lira to his name. Every penny I earned would have gone into trying to keep up his grotty castello.' She sighed reminiscently. 'But until the plane landed at Heathrow this morning I was certain I was madly in love with him.'

'And what happened then?'

'I realised there was a great deal to be said for Richard and his Mercedes,' Sacha said candidly.

Fran laughed and Sacha re-filled her glass and went on coaxingly, 'Now come on and tell me everything that's been happening. Not the details that are sacred between husband and wife, of course, but a general picture plus a heavy hint or two.'

They talked for some time. Fran kept her contributions light, reluctant to reveal everything was not perfect. She made no mention of the unwelcome press coverage, and Sacha knew nothing about it since she had been away when it happened. They were just beginning to wind down and Fran was considering ringing Grant when the doorbell went.

Sacha pulled a face as she got up to answer it, but she gave a squeal as she opened the door and exclaimed, 'How lovely! Go and see who I've already got here!' and Fran looked up enquiringly to see Libby and Seth shedding their coats as they came into the room.

Libby was considerably more pregnant than she had expected. She must have shown her surprise because Seth grinned and said, 'Don't worry—it's all legal now.'

'That must be a relief for Libby,' Fran observed. She gave her a mildly apologetic glance. 'I'd somehow got the impression that the event was rather more in the mists of the future.'

Libby said breezily, 'A slight miscalculation in the beginning, then it took me another month to get round to telling Seth.' She settled herself into the corner of the settee, obviously unconcerned by her advanced condition since she hadn't bothered to shroud the bulge in a smock. 'But don't bother to humour him—he's over the shock now.'

'Yeah,' Seth agreed. 'It's good for the tax situation. I was keeping her before anyway. Now it's cheaper.'

'And don't be fooled,' Libby added. 'He's not as cynical as he sounds. Sacha, love, I could murder a cup of tea—can I beg one? I'm off coffee and alcohol and I'm dying of thirst.'

Always restless, she struggled to the edge of the settee to get up again, and Seth leaned forward and lifted her easily by her elbow. He did it unconsciously, which Fran felt was a good sign, and when Libby had followed Sacha into the kitchen she smiled up at him. 'Has the thought of fatherhood lost its terrors?'

'Almost,' he admitted. 'She's a good kid really, or so her mother keeps telling me. Irons a real cool shirt.' He paused and smiled back at her. 'And how's life with you? Your husband beating you yet?'

'No, but he might start if I don't ring him soon,' Fran said. It occurred to her for the first time to wonder how Grant would react to finding Seth there, and she felt a stirring of unease. It might be better if she went down and waited for him outside. To her annoyance she found she was feeling guilty, as though she really had got something to hide, and a faint rebellion awoke in her. It was the first time she had been out in the evening on her own, whereas Grant had left her several times and she had only his word that he had been where he said he was going.

She had half-risen from her chair, but she sank back again and listened with amusement to the conversation issuing from the kitchen. Sacha's current craze was health foods and she was extolling the virtues of herbal tea, which appeared to be the only kind she had in the place. Libby, inclined to be forthright, gave her opinion of it, and came back into the lounge resignedly clutching a glass of lemon squash.

'And you're lucky to get even that,' Fran informed her. 'It's been here since I left.'

'It keeps, darling,' Sacha soothed. She emptied the last of the wine into Seth's glass, filling it to the brim, and went to open another bottle. She couldn't find room for it on the table when she got back, so she stood it on the shelf next to the clock, and Seth told her amiably that the place was a tip. Sacha pointed out his own shortcomings, and while they were arguing, Libby quietly went to sleep. After a while Sacha noticed and raised her eyebrows in astonishment, and Seth grinned.

'It's all right, she does it all the time. It's getting late though, so I'd better wake her.'

He got to his feet and Fran realised with a jolt that it was nearly midnight. She must have somehow misread her watch the last time she looked at it. She was conscious of a feeling of relief at the thought that at least Seth would be gone when Grant came for her now, but at that moment the bell went again, and with sinking feeling she knew this would be Grant.

CHAPTER SEVEN

SETH let him in and he stood just inside the door, not bothering to smile as he looked round at them all and then round the room.

Fran looked as well, and saw how it would appear to him—the bottles and glasses and cigarette smoke—one of Sacha's discordant records playing in the background. She was smoking herself, which she hadn't done for months, but Seth had offered her one and she had accepted it, mainly because she thought she might just as well inhale her own smoke as his.

Still unsmiling, Grant said, 'It was getting late so I came for you anyway.'

He remained standing where he was, obviously waiting for her, and Fran said quickly, 'Come and sit down for a moment. You can't walk straight in and straight out again, and you haven't met Seth's wife, Libby yet, have you?'

She was babbling. She could hear the nervous inflection in her voice herself, and realised she was afraid of Grant saying something cutting, and spoiling for the others what had been a very innocent, enjoyable evening. With relief she noticed the lines in his face became less rigid. Responding to the unconscious plea in her expression he acknowledged the introduction and even accepted a drink from Sacha when she waved the wine bottle at him in casual invitation. Afterwards he stood talking to Seth and Fran gradually relaxed when it seemed they were getting on well enough, amicably comparing the changes that the acquisition of a wife had made in their lives.

'Do you reckon they realise how lucky they are to have caught us?' Seth demanded, gesturing towards Libby with his wine glass. By no means drunk, he was nevertheless a little mellow, enough to make him incautious, and he missed the sardonic light in Grant's eyes as they slid over Libby's expanding shape before returning to his face.

'Oh, I'm certain Libby realises it,' Grant returned, smoothly cynical.

'Yeah, but you've got to keep reminding them of it regularly,' Seth insisted. 'Otherwise they start taking you for granted. I mean you sure came along at just the right moment for Fran, so keep her on her toes—tell her how lucky she is every day over breakfast, that's my advice to you.'

Smiling still, Grant was suddenly alert. His voice deceptively casual, he enquired, 'How did I come along at just the right moment?'

Seth hitched himself round to lean more comfortably on the back of the settee. 'I was scraping the barrel for her,' he admitted frankly. He gave a mournful shake of his head. 'You know, it's an odd thing, this business. You get some girl come along and you wouldn't even call her good looking, yet she's got something that comes across—photographs like a dream. Then there's Fran here, seems to have everything when you look at her—beautiful, got the high cheekbones, the lot, and she comes out like Miss Piggy.'

'Darling, I wouldn't stand for that!' Sacha exclaimed, outraged. 'Tell him!'

But Fran couldn't, held mute by impending disaster as Grant pursued quietly, 'But I thought you told me she could have had a brilliant career.'

'Oh, she could have done,' Seth assured him. 'She'd still have been at the top even now if she'd taken my advice and stripped off in the early days. I'd have made a pile from my twenty per cent.' He drained his glass with a flourish and put it down on the table beside him, then shook his head again. 'She changed her mind too late though, and of course that operation finished her chances. There's not much you can do to hide a scar like that—no good even to the bra and briefs customer now. Pity, because I'm sure I was right. With that last set of photographs I've got we'd have had them fighting for her.'

There was total, electrified silence as he smiled reminiscently and drew on his cigarette. Fran knew he was the only one in the room unaware of the violent menace behind Grant's sudden stillness.

She cried out quickly, 'Grant . . .!' but he ignored her, and said softly, 'I want them.'

'Eh?'

'I want them,' Grant repeated with the same soft savagery. 'Those photographs—I want them now!'

Seth awoke belatedly to his own danger. 'Hey, don't get the wrong idea,' he said protestingly. 'This is advertising, man! Shower units, bathtubs, deodorants, the new magic formula that dissolves away the hairs on your legs instantly!—Women's glossies stuff! Hell, Fran,' he appealed. 'Tell him I run a respectable business, will you? I'm not into girlie mags and peddling porn!'

'I'll hear what she has to say later,' Grant told him. His voice was glacial, and Fran felt the threat in it transferred to herself. 'But first I want those photographs. Where are they?'

Giving up the fight, Seth said, 'Down at the agency office in the files. You'll have to drive. I should get breathalysed.'

Mortally afraid for him, Fran said, 'Give me the keys and I'll get them. I know where they are.'

Grant merely said, 'No,' without looking at her, and

she subsided, too frightened for herself as well to risk enraging him further.

There were two quite separate and distinct reasons for his fury, she knew. One was that the photographs existed at all, and remembering his reaction to a neckline he considered too revealing she shivered, because the one would have been enough in itself. The second reason was that Seth still had them. With an ounce of the self-preservation the wine had robbed him of he would have realised his mistake and said instantly that they had been destroyed, or at least claimed that he had forgotten them. As it was, he had betrayed that he knew perfectly well that they were still there, four months after her operation—four months after any usefulness had been killed.

She saw him suddenly realise and sober up. She hoped he was sober enough to think of some convincing explanation on the way to the office, because frankly she couldn't herself.

Nobody said a word as he put on his sheepskin coat and felt in the pocket to make sure he had the keys. He and Grant went out, and the silence lingered until they heard the Daimler start up below the window. Then Sacha said in a careful voice, 'I think you may have a teeny bit more than you can handle there, sweetie. Your old bed is still vacant if you'd rather give tempers time to cool and deal with it in the morning.'

Fran's stomach was palpitating with fright and she daren't look at Libby. She was almost certain that Grant would never physically harm a woman, but he was unlikely to exercise the same restraint when it came to Seth. She said, 'Thanks for the offer, but I think he'll calm down when he actually sees the portfolio. With any luck Seth will have the sense to show him a few of the others in the files, then he'll realise they're absolutely standard.'

Caustically, Sacha said, 'It's a pity Seth didn't realise before he opened his big mouth that what is just shop talk to us might sound very different to a husband who's not in the trade.'

For Libby's sake they were both skirting round the fact that the portfolio should have been scrapped, but Fran knew that Sacha was speculating as well on how Grant could have remained so long in ignorance of the true facts about her former career.

She made no comment, however, merely saying, 'Well let's try to create a slightly better impression for when they get back.'

Opening the window six inches, she gathered up the full ashtrays and a handful of glasses and took them into the kitchen. Fran and Libby collected up the rest, and when they had wiped the tables and straightened the cushions the place was comparatively presentable and free from smoke. They were all listening for the car's return, and when it stopped outside, Fran picked up her jacket and bag. 'On second thoughts it might be better if Grant didn't come back in.' She gave them both a wan, apologetic smile. 'Sorry to have wrecked the evening.'

Libby gave her a feeble, suspicious smile in return, and with an assumption of lightness, Sacha said, 'All that tidying up for nothing. Well, scream if you need any help, darling, and give me a ring when you can.'

Fran nodded and made a hurried exit. She passed Seth on the half-landing and was relieved to see that though his face was grim there was no outward sign of damage. She couldn't summon the courage to look at Grant.

Nothing was said until they were in the car, then he paused before switching on the ignition and ordered harshly, 'In future stay away from Bernstein!'

He started up the engine before she could reply, and

she made no attempt to defend herself until they were in the apartment. Then, she said desperately, 'Grant, I know what you're thinking, but you're wrong.'

'Am I?' His face taut with rage, he took his coat off and flung it on to a nearby chair, unheeding when it slid off and fell to the floor. 'But then you don't know what I *am* thinking, do you?'

'Seth isn't . . .' she began, but he cut in on her violently.

'I don't want to hear!'

He swung away from her and rubbed his clenched fist across the back of his neck for a moment, then turned round to face her again and repeated more quietly, 'I don't want to hear. I've never asked you about him and I'm not asking now—you would deny it anyway.' He drew a deep breath, and when he spoke again his voice was all the more deadly for its rigid control. 'But no man, with my knowledge, keeps photographs of my wife to look at and gloat over in secret. He had no reason to hold on to them, apart from his own private gratification, and you know that as well as I do. So stay away from him! For his sake as well as yours!'

He picked up the Scotch bottle and unscrewed the cap. Pouring himself a generous measure, he cradled the glass in his hands and leaned against the sideboard, watching her broodingly. 'You asked me why I was marrying you, but I never asked you that same question. It seems I should have done.' He gave a short laugh. 'But you were hardly likely to tell me you were broke and out of a job . . .'

Momentarily his mouth twisted in distaste, and Fran burst out, 'I *wasn't* broke and I *had* got a job!'

'Doing what?'

'I was a beauty counsellor. I demonstrated make-up in a store.'

Contemptuously, he said, 'Are you asking me to

believe you were satisfied with that after the sort of life you'd led before?' His voice harsh, he went on, 'You'd been used to something very different; premières and parties, mixing with people who had money, living in an expensive flat, then suddenly you were a sales assistant.' He took a mouthful of the amber liquid in his glass. 'And your lover had inconveniently got another girl pregnant and was out of the running. I certainly did come along at just the right moment for you, didn't I?'

'No!'

She almost shouted it, and he made an impatient sound and slammed his glass down on the sideboard. 'You took damned good care I never discovered any of this at the time.'

'It wasn't like that! I *wasn't* deliberately hiding it from you!'

He stared across at her, his eyes hooded, then said abruptly, 'All right. Why *did* you marry me?'

'I . . .' Under his gaze, she swallowed and fell silent. There couldn't possibly be a worse moment for telling him she loved him—she cringed at the thought of his sneering disbelief. 'I think we both had the same reason,' she said at last.

Grant sent her a humourless smile. 'So nothing is really changed. We've both still got what we wanted. And you give value for money, darling, I'll grant you that. I hope I never disappoint in my turn.'

He walked towards her, and Fran felt a sick excitement as she read his intention in his eyes. She backed away from him wordlessly, then turned and ran out of the room, realising her mistake when he caught her before she could slam the bedroom door against him.

Hauling her towards him, he pinned her arms to her sides and said, 'I agree—it's more comfortable in bed,' and brought his mouth down on hers, forcing her lips savagely apart.

At first she fought him. It was an instinctive reaction against being physically overpowered, but then she wondered why she was doing it. She loved him, and in refusing him she could destroy her one hold on him. His desire for her was the only thing she could be certain of, the only thing which might keep him with her long enough to learn he was wrong about her. As her resistance ceased, the pressure of his lips softened and became coaxing, insidiously compelling a response from her, and she sighed when he drew away.

His eyes narrowed in a smile, he studied her flushed face, and murmured, 'What a good job, darling, that you're as much of a sensualist as I am,' and smothered her resentment with his mouth again, while his hand slid beneath her sweater to find her breast. He was an expert, and completely attuned to her by now, teasing and tormenting her to unashamed arousal as he removed her clothes and then his own. By the time he lowered her to the bed she was ready for him, her body inviting him with its own silent language, and her arms closed round him hungrily as he took slow possession of her.

But immediately she realised it was not his intention to bring her to a swift release. His leisured movements kept her on the edge but would take her no further, and his own mouth rigid with the strain of self-control, he watched the agony of frustration twist her expression, slowing his pace still more and giving her a glittering smile when she began to whimper and plead with him to end it.

Shaking his head he said, 'No,' and brought his mouth down until she could feel the warmth of his breath on her ear. 'No, darling, not yet,' he repeated with soft vehemence. 'I'm going to make this something you'll never forget.'

There was a kind of menace in the muted assertion,

but she was so far gone under his erotic mastery that nothing could reverse the fevered advance of her body's responses. She twisted and moved against him frenziedly in an effort to overcome his restraint, then began to rail at him because he knew the torture he was inflicting with his denial and his smile showed he rejoiced in it. Enraged, she sank her teeth into his arm and heard his grunt of pain and half-muffled obscenity as he grabbed her hair, wrenching at it to force her to let go.

Either her attack caused him to relax his control or he was persuaded she could endure no more, but at last he brought her fiercely to the conclusion she so desperately craved. It was so intense when it came that her body remained locked, and for endless moments she was frozen into a blackness like death, unable to draw air into her starved lungs. Then her muscles relaxed and she took a long, gasping breath, aware now of Grant pressing her down by her shoulders, murmuring to her and soothing.

Dazed, she turned her head to look at him, then closed her eyes against the unhidden triumph in his expression. He had achieved what he set out to do and he was exultant. By an act of total, physical domination he had brought her to a pitch of sensation which could never be surpassed, but she knew with sudden clarity that she never wanted to experience it again. Not in the same way. He had reduced it to a purely sexual act—a matter only of electrified nerves and unbearably stimulated senses. Without tenderness and human warmth it was joyless.

He had done it to avenge himself. After reducing her to abject pleading, and proving to her that he would always hold the control, he had deliberately set out to erase the memories he thought she carried from her past, raising her to such a height that he knew nothing could compare with it. And doubtless, if there had been anything to compare, he would have succeeded. His pride and his male jealousy were now appeased, but she wondered wistfully what he would say if she told him that now it was over it meant nothing—that she would gladly surrender all the heights if he would only look at her with the same expression in his eyes as in that smiling photograph with Julia.

He continued to hold her until her hips were strained and her body ached from his weight; not with the languid pleasure of former times, but as though he was reminding her of his ownership. The discomfort eventually became too much and she pushed at his shoulders with her hands. At once he withdrew from her and rolled away, reaching over to switch off the lights. As she pulled the quilt up round her, he said, 'We're going home at the weekend,' and a cold fear settled on her, but this time she dared make no protest.

It wasn't until she opened her bag for a handkerchief the following day that she recalled the letter she had picked up. The contents sent her flying to ring Sacha, but there was no reply, and in panic she went to see Seth.

His face was a study when she pushed open his office door. For a split second he regarded her with stupefied disbelief, then he exploded out of his chair, scattering papers from the desk.

'For God's sake, have you got a death wish?' he demanded incredulously. He slammed the door behind her, breathing heavily. 'You're out of your mind coming here!'

Disjointedly, she said, 'I'm sorry but I had to. Seth, I'm in trouble.'

'Darling, I've got troubles of my own.' Seth put both hands up to his eyes, rubbing them wearily before he collapsed behind his desk again. 'I had a question and answers session with Libby that went on half the night, and the last thing I need on top of it is for your husband to try to spread me over the walls. He carries more weight than I do, and he might just possibly succeed. Stay away, Fran—stick to the phone, and preferably not your own even then. Now for both our sakes, get going before he finds you here.'

She shook her head. 'He wouldn't think I'd come.'

'I wouldn't have done either, which proves something,' Seth muttered. 'Darling, *he's* coming here! He wanted the negatives of those photographs and he's collecting them in an hour.'

Fran made an instinctive movement towards the door, then checked as her mind began to function again. 'I'll be gone in five minutes. Seth, I've got to have a hundred pounds at once. Can you lend it to me?'

Amazement blending with suspicion in his voice, he said, 'Your husband's not short of a hundred quid. What in hell's name do you want it for that you can't ask him?'

'Oh God, Seth, I couldn't ask him for anything at the moment.' She sank down on to the chair opposite him, fighting to hold back tears. 'I'm overdrawn at the bank. It's from before we were married—I must have added up wrongly or something when I was out shopping and I've only just found out. I forgot to give the bank my new name and address so the mail went to Sacha's and she's been away.'

Seth was staring at her, nonplussed, and in agony she went on, 'I *can't* let him find out, Seth, not after last night and with what he thinks already!'

'What's happened to your brains?' Seth enquired. 'You used to be quite a bright girl. Darling, the bank isn't going to dun Mrs Grant Mercier for a paltry hundred quid. Relax. Pay them back out of your housekeeping. They'll wait.'

Only half-convinced, she said, 'But Grant uses the same bank. Are you sure there's no way he could find out?'

'They're separate accounts,' he said patiently. 'Just don't leave your statements lying around, that's all.'

'Yes. Yes, of course. I've never been overdrawn before and I'm not thinking very clearly this morning. Coming on top of those photographs . . .'

Morosely, he said, 'Yeah, I put my foot in it all round, but how was I to know you'd never said anything about them? If it's any comfort to you, Libby's giving me hell. I told her I'd forgotten to chuck them out of the files but she doesn't believe me either. She thinks I still lust after you.' He sent her a crooked smile. 'True, of course.'

'But you never really . . .' she began, then stopped short as she met his eyes.

'No,' he agreed. 'Not much point, was there, when it was so obvious I didn't turn you on.'

Acutely uncomfortable, Fran stared at him, not knowing what to reply. It came to her suddenly that he was the one man she might have responded to if she had known he was serious. She wished she hadn't realised it. In some curious way it made her feel guilty, and any attempt now to make Grant believe he was no more than a friend would be robbed of its conviction.

She said finally, 'I wish you hadn't told me,' and he shrugged.

'If I didn't do anything about it before I'm not going to now.'

'No.' Embarrassed and anxious to be away, she picked up her bag from the desk, then asked, 'What did Grant say when you came down here last night?'

'Didn't he tell you?'

When she shook her head he gave her an odd look and said lightly, 'We didn't talk a lot. He offered to break my neck for me, which I thought was over-reacting a bit, but it didn't seem the moment to argue about it. There wasn't much else apart from the business of getting the negatives back.'

Hesitantly, Fran said, 'Then you haven't told him what you said at the hospital that time . . . well, that it was all rubbish.'

He looked at her with pure astonishment. 'I didn't think I needed to. After what you said, I rather assumed he'd have found it out for himself by now.'

'Unfortunately, contrary to popular belief, the evidence isn't always indisputable.' She flushed slightly. 'I did a lot of riding when I was younger which probably accounts for it.'

With a groan, Seth buried his head in his hands, then looked back at her and said grimly, 'I suppose I should be grateful that he only offered to break it. Darling, there's a thing called verbal communication which you don't seem to have heard of, but if I were you I should try it.'

'He's not likely to believe anything I say after last night.' She fiddled with the clasp on her bag, feeling tears come to her eyes again, and said stonily, 'He thinks I married him because I had to give up modelling and I was broke. That's why I panicked when I found out about the hundred pounds.'

Regarding her helplessly, Seth said, 'If you don't get out of here soon it isn't going to matter what he thinks.'

The reminder brought her to her feet with a resurgence of fright, and his expression wry, he said, 'Do me a favour, darling—don't come back again. Your husband's bigger and fitter than I am, and I've already got enough on my hands with Libby. Her hormones are all to hell at the moment.'

As she left, Fran was filled with remorse for having involved him. It had seemed a harmless enough

deception when she asked him to do it for her, but it
had proved to have unforeseen consequences for both
of them. Making her way to the bank she was haunted
by the phrase about tangled webs. She should take
more notice of the warnings in some of the old adages.

When she arrived at the bank she found Seth had been
right in his assessment. They were completely unconcerned, and if only she'd had the sense to ring up and
explain she would have saved herself a traumatic couple
of hours. She paid in twenty pounds, then went home,
nervously hoping Grant would still be out so that she
needn't think up excuses for where she had been.

He was waiting for her, and she knew at once that
excuses were useless. As she registered the unconcealed
rage in his face he said harshly, 'I told you to keep away
from him!'

Poised by the door she could feel his anger vibrating
over her. Her stomach lurched with fear, but she made
herself advance slowly into the room. 'I just wanted to
find what had been said last night, that's all.' Half-
pleadingly, she added, 'Seth didn't know I was going.'

'Fortunately for him, I realised that.' He paused,
surveying her grimly. 'If he'd known about your visit
he'd have had the sense to warn his receptionist to keep
her mouth shut in advance. As it was, I got to her
before he could.' Miraculously his anger seemed to
dissipate, and with weary contempt, he said, 'Leave the
poor bastard alone, Fran. Give his wife a chance at
least, even if you haven't got any pity for him.'

Stung, Fran flared, 'I only went to see him for a few
minutes in his office. That hardly amounts to seducing
him away from Libby!'

'For God's sake, haven't you got *any* imagination?'
he demanded, anger rising again. 'They might have
married because she was pregnant but the poor kid
loves him—that's obvious! How do you think she must

feel knowing he was forced into it and it's you he really wants? You don't need to actually sleep with him to wreck that set-up.'

For a while Fran was held silent by the undeniable truth of his assertion. Her voice muffled, she said at last, 'They'll be all right. Perhaps Seth doesn't love her in the same way, but he's very fond of her. He wouldn't do anything to hurt her.'

'And you honestly believe that is enough? That a marriage can still be happy even though all the love is only on one side?'

Shocked by the raw bitterness in his voice, Fran's eyes flew to his face he swung away from her.

'It isn't enough, believe me!' With sudden, violent intensity, he declared, 'It's a recipe for heartbreak and regret!'

His words seemed to beat non-stop into Fran's brain as she went about the preparations for their departure. She suspected they even wove themselves into her dreams, oppressing her before the moment of waking, enveloping her in a grey blanket of foreboding. Grant hadn't been referring to their marriage at the time—his bitter statement has sprung from his own past experience, but it applied equally well to them. It wasn't enough for only one to love.

After his outbreak of rage he was distant, spending most of his time in his study, but he still reached for her in the night, and once, encouraged by the dark and physical closeness, she tried to explain to him how she had never mentioned her failure in modelling because she hadn't realised it could ever have any significance— that it had seemed unimportant, irrelevant, and her mind was too concentrated on the future.

When she had finished, Grant said, 'But you must have realised I was under the impression that you had a successful career.'

'It didn't even occur to me. We got married so quickly that there wasn't much time for talking. Afterwards we never discussed the past.' She turned her head towards him and reminded with a trace of challenge, 'You've never discussed the past either.'

'No,' he admitted after a pause.

'Do you believe me?'

He moved restlessly, silent with his thoughts, and said eventually, 'If you want me to give you a definite yes or no, I can't. It isn't as clear-cut and straightforward as that. Until now I've judged on events and in the light of how they appeared to me. I have to say that it still seems the only logical way to reach a conclusion and I shall go on doing it. So—it's up to you.'

It was a small hope—half a hope. At least he hadn't given her an outright no. She said quietly, 'There's one thing which I can never prove to you, so I'll just have to ask you to accept it as the truth. I'd already decided before my operation not to go in for nude modelling.'

'Why, if it was likely to be so lucrative?'

There was a hard edge to his voice again, and she grimaced, even though he couldn't see her. 'I'm afraid it wasn't for the only reason you would consider valid. When you've been in the business for a few years, taking your clothes off for a photographer doesn't bother you provided he's a genuine professional, and Seth wouldn't have sent me out to anyone who wasn't. It was just that I was never keen on the job in the first place. It's insecure and boring, and I was sick of fending off men who'd got the wrong idea. It was beyond a joke already, and I knew it was bound to get worse.'

His voice totally without expression, he commented, 'You didn't do much fending off where I was concerned.'

Fran felt a rush of heat rise up her neck and face. 'I didn't actually need to call a halt with you,' she pointed out constrictedly.

'You mean you'd have applied the brakes before we reached the ultimate? A dangerous game to play when a man's in a state of high sexual arousal. As I'm sure you must have known.'

'Not from personal experience.'

She felt his head turn swiftly in her direction, and in a low voice, went on, 'No one had made love to me to that extent before.'

He tensed beside her, then said flatly, 'The evidence is against you, darling. I'm well aware that the signs aren't always present, but if you had been a virgin you wouldn't have waited until now to tell me.' Almost indifferently, he added, 'I wasn't expecting to find one anyway.'

In other words, why waste my time trying to convince you, Fran thought wearily. Concentrate on the claims I have a better chance of proving.

But her faint hope of succeeding gradually died as the weekend drew nearer. On Saturday they were going home. Back to the house Grant had shared with Julia, where all her own shortcomings and inadequacies would be magnified—where his disillusionment would finally be complete and he would be compelled to acknowledge to himself that he had acquired an inferior imitation. Like an art reproduction, pleasing enough in a suburban living room, she would seem shoddy in the setting which had once housed the original.

It was overcast and cold when they arrived. Grant drove the car close up to the front door to unload the luggage, then took it round to the garage at the back. For a while Fran waited for him on the steps, reluctant to greet Mrs Matthews on her own, then decided she was being craven and went into the hall.

Aggressive barking startled her, and two Jack Russells skidded round a corner to confront her. They were both strange to her, young and smooth-haired, but in their wake, slow and stiff-legged, came the one she remembered. With a wary eye on the other two Fran bent down and called her, and Ruff advanced unwillingly, her elderly face suspicious and unfriendly. She sniffed Fran's outstretched hand for a moment, then turned away, uninterested, and quick tears blurred Fran's gaze. Ruff didn't remember her.

She stood up again and wished she had waited for Grant when she saw Mrs Matthews watching her from the far end of the hall, her manner as unfriendly as Ruff's had been. Uncomfortable and uncertain how to address her, Fran waited, hoping the other woman would speak, then said, 'Hello, Mrs Matthews.'

After a short pause, the housekeeper said deliberately, 'Hello, Fran.'

Her flat tone and the use of Fran's first name had been intentional, to put her at a disadvantage, subtly reversing the role of employer and employee. In an attempt to counteract it, Fran said casually, 'Grant will be here in a moment—he's just gone to put the car away. Perhaps we could have some coffee. It's been a long journey.'

Mrs Matthews said, 'I've already taken the tray into the sitting room,' and Fran felt the malice behind her words. She didn't know where the sitting room was, as the other woman well knew. Determined not to ask she stayed silent until Mrs Matthews said grudgingly, 'I'll show you the way.'

She shook her head then, and said, 'No, it's quite all right, I'll wait for Grant.'

The dogs greeted him ecstatically, the two young ones racing madly round the hall, unable to contain their excitement, while Ruff quivered at his feet, her stump of a tail wagging furiously. Laughing as he gave them all a final pat, he said, 'Sorry, Matty, I should have said hello to you first. How are you?'

Unbending slightly, Mrs Matthews said, 'Well enough, Mr Grant,' adding, 'I've taken your coffee in,' as he picked up the suitcases again.

'Right, I'll have it first then.' He dumped the cases and Fran followed him into the room where the tray rested on a polished dark wood table. The housekeeper came too, but smoothly and pleasantly, Fran said, 'It's all right, Mrs Matthews, I'll see to it.'

The older woman sent her a glance which was perilously close to a glare, and when she had gone out, Grant said, 'Try to be a bit tactful with her at first. She's known you from a child so it's a slightly awkward situation.'

'I appreciate that, but perhaps you could tell her the same thing.'

Fran's reply came more sharply than she had intended, and she saw Grant frown before she turned away from him to pour the coffee. She took her cup over to the window and gazed out over the valley to the village on the far side. Normally the forge and her uncle's house would be visible from here, but it had begun to drizzle and a misty greyness obliterated the familiar scene. It had been a dismal day in London, but somehow the trees in the square outside the flat had never seemed as desolate as the view from this window now.

She let her eyes stray round the room instead. The embroidered satin cushion covers would be Julia's work, of course, the silver grey exactly right against the dark blue velvet of the suite, the blue embroidery a perfect match. She would have made the satin lampshade as well, with its discreet blue and silver trim.

She set her cup down so quickly that it rattled. Grant turned his head quickly at the sound and said, 'I'll take the luggage up then show you round.'

She nodded and tried to make her stiff facial muscles show some sign of enthusiasm. The rest of the house would be just as beautiful as this room and he would expect her to display pleasure in her new home. She couldn't let him know that she felt none—that the elegant room repelled her and made her feel an intruder, uninvited and unwanted.

She followed him on the tour with ever-lowering spirits. Julia was everywhere. When they reached the kitchen she stood in the doorway and silently stared round. This was where she had sat drinking her Coke with Grant all those years ago. Her memory of it was as sharp as though it had been yesterday, but nothing remained. Fitted units lined the wall once occupied by the old, solid fuel cooker, and the quarried floor was replaced by smooth, honey brown tiles. A hanging basket of plants trailed down luxuriantly beside the breakfast table in the alcove. Mrs Matthews had tended it lovingly for her departed mistress, Fran thought, her eyes dwelling on the glossy leaves.

The coldness inside her increasing, she accompanied Grant round the first floor. There were four other rooms apart from their own and Mrs Matthews' sitting room and bedroom. They were all large and airy and tastefully decorated, two of them with fourposters, though not as intricately carved as the one in their own room which Grant showed to her last. Julia had chosen red and cream in here—a thick, pale carpet, and the looped-back curtains of the bed and windows in a deep, jewel red.

She couldn't say anything. If she had spoken it would have been a frantic plea to Grant to take her away from here—back to London, anywhere away from the presence in this room she was expected to share with him. She even imagined she could smell her perfume still lingering in the carpet and fabrics where she had sat and walked and touched things. People often claimed they could smell perfume in haunted houses, but Julia wasn't dead, Fran thought wildly. She was alive—as alive as if she had only stepped out of this room the moment before they themselves entered.

She looked at the bed and was overcome with the same sickness she had felt when she had gone into the bedroom of the apartment before they were married. Only this time there would be no deliverance. This time she would lie in the bed and *know* she was resting on the same mattress, her head on the same pillow, her body beneath Grant's in the place where he had embraced Julia in the same extremity of passion.

Bile rose in her throat and she went into the bathroom and filled a toothmug with water to wash it down again. When she got back Grant had unlocked the cases and was hanging his own things in the wardrobe. She said, 'I'll do that,' and he relinquished them to her.

'Thanks. There are several people I have to ring, and I want to get myself organised in my study.'

Already he was involved, picking up his life from a few months before as though he had never been away. He would check on his horses and the farm, talk with his manager and his other friends, while she . . . what would she do? She could go down and help with the dinner, but her help wasn't needed and she would merely expose herself as a moderate and inexperienced cook before a woman who was ill-disposed towards her.

She opened up her own cases and crossed the room to inspect the other wardrobe. As she opened the doors, perfume wafted out strongly and she knew she hadn't imagined it before. There were only some blankets

stored in a drawer, and primarily they had a clean,
washed smell so it wasn't those. Perfume couldn't
possibly linger for three years, and her lips tightening
she went back to the bathroom and looked in the
mirrored cabinets. As she had half-expected there was a
partly used flagon of Arpège. A little welcoming gesture
from Mrs Matthews, she thought bitterly.

When she went downstairs the dogs barked at her
again, one of them growling threateningly when she
tried to make overtures. Grant told her they were four
when she asked him later on. So even the dogs would
owe loyalty to her predecessor.

Dinner that night was excellent. Proffering an olive
branch, Fran went to congratulate Mrs Matthews on
the meal, but there was no lessening of hostility, and
depressed, she went back to the sitting room where
Grant was watching a current events programme on the
television. The two young dogs were settled comfortably
at his feet, but Ruff scratched at his leg, pleading to be
allowed up beside him, and after a while, Fran said,
'Why don't you have her up?'

He rubbed his hand ruefully along the white, rough-
coated back. 'She'll smother the settee in hairs.'

'They'll brush off,' Fran pointed out.

'If I let Ruff on the others will come as well,' he
warned. 'Won't you mind?'

'If you have dogs you expect dog hairs,' she said,
faintly surprised. 'It's the penalty you pay for the
pleasure of their company.'

He continued to regard her for a few seconds longer,
then suddenly smiled and clicked his fingers to Ruff.
She jumped up immediately and rested her chin on his
leg with a long sigh of contentment. The other dogs
raised their heads, and Grant said, 'Come the other side
while the space is still vacant.'

He was offering her an olive branch, she realised.

With a rush of gladness she went into his encircling arm and for a while they watched the television, then his arm tightened and he turned his head to kiss her. His mouth on hers was light but lingering, a half-serious precursor to the lovemaking he anticipated later. Normally it would have aroused a warmth in her, and an equal readiness for what was to follow.

But now there was nothing. Her mind had gone on ahead, picturing the room upstairs, the big fourposter with its luxurious cover, and Julia, her long hair spread loose across the pillow where she herself would be laying her head that night. The image was so clear it might have been something she had actually witnessed. It took hold of her mind, excluding all other thought, cancelling out the message to her brain that Grant's lips were sending, crowding out her reaction to the gentle caress of his hand on her breast.

He lifted his head, and his expression faintly enquiring, said, 'Tired?'

She nodded. 'Travelling always wears me out. I don't know why. Sitting there while someone else drives is hardly energetic.'

'Go to bed. I'll just watch the end of this, then I'll let the dogs out and lock up.'

She fell in with his suggestion but mounted the stairs slowly, unwilling to face the alien aura in the bedroom again. It would be better once this first night was over, she told herself. She *was* tired, and she had a nagging backache—she was letting everything affect her too much, and she would just have to learn to get over this revulsion. The temptation to pretend to be asleep when Grant came up was strong but she quelled it, then discovered the cause of the backache and realised circumstances had relieved her of the decision. With an ironic smile she donned one of her little-used nightdresses, and summoning all her resolution, climbed into the high bed.

It was worse than she had imagined. For a while she lay there, breathing in the faint but persistent scent of Arpège, then abruptly got out and opened the window. The night air chilled the room, but anything was better than that cloying suffocation. Trying to settle she switched off the light, but pictures formed in the darkness, scourging her, and she turned it on again. Through the open window she heard Grant quietly calling the dogs in, a nightly ritual that would soon be as familiar to her as it had been to Julia. No, not soon. Julia had been married to him for six years. Would she feel secure when she had reached that magic target herself? When she could notch up seven years, eight years, could she relax in the knowledge that she had passed her rival's score?

She was locked in a rigid tension when Grant came in. He spoke her name softly and she counterfeited a sleepy murmur in reply and lay listening as he got ready for bed. He got in beside her, then said wryly, 'Oh,' as his hand encountered the silk of her nightdress. Resting his hand on her hip, he kissed the back of her neck and whispered, 'That was bad timing. Tonight should have been our house-warming.'

She said sharply, 'It's always bad timing as far as you're concerned.'

There was a pause and he removed his hand and rolled on to his back. 'True,' he agreed in a colourless voice. 'But until now I always thought it was a view we shared.'

She could have bitten her tongue out for that acid retort. She said quickly, 'I'm sorry, I didn't mean it. I feel a bit low and I'm touchy. Mrs Matthews rather got to me. She's never going to accept me . . .' Hastily she broke off, but she saw Grant's brows draw together and knew she might just as well have said, 'In place of Julia.'

'She's been here over twenty years and she's near retiring age. You'll have to make allowances—give her time to get used to you.'

'All right.' Fran tried to keep the stiffness from her voice, hiding her resentment that all the allowances were to be on her side only. It seemed that Mrs Matthews rated more consideration in his eyes than she did. She realised she was being childish, but a small core of grievance stayed with her as she settled down once more to try to sleep.

It stayed with her throughout the days which followed. Mrs Matthews continued to treat her with barely veiled contempt, and she had the household and the two dailies under her complete control. Fran insisted on washing her own clothes and Grant's, but it did little to fill her time, and sorting out cupboards and attics only brought fresh reminders of Julia. Several, she suspected, had been placed there deliberately—the photographs, some taken with Grant, some of Julia alone, a box of recipe cards in her clear, sloping writing, jigsaw puzzles of flowers and country gardens, a half-completed cushion cover matching those in the sitting room. She left them where she found them, but resolved that the first time Mrs Matthews took a holiday, out they would all go.

Since she had no transport until Grant brought her car from London, Ralph, the groom, dropped her in the village a few times to see her aunt and uncle. They were happy to see her, but she couldn't go too often, and in a desperate attempt to combat her boredom she began to teach herself to play the piano. The instrument was an impressive grand and she felt presumptuous as she practised scales and exercises from a tutor she found in the stool. Grant was a good pianist and grimaced at the discordant sounds she produced, but she persisted, undeterred.

He was taking the train to London in order to drive her car back, and Fran stood on the step to wave him off as he went with Ralph to the station. She watched as he stopped in the narrow lane to speak to the postman and receive his letters through the open window, then the postman plodded on up the slope. There was only one letter, a long brown envelope from the bank. Opening it she gave a cursory glance at the statement, then read it again, puzzled. It took a second for her to realise that it was Grant's name on the top, then she went cold. If the postman had given hers to Grant and he also opened it without noticing he would see that damning overdraft and the original date of it, all neatly printed out to confirm his suspicions.

For a moment she was too shaken to take in anything else, then the recurring standing order caught her eye. She read it with disbelief, then a gathering icy rage. If Grant could afford to give that amount to his ex-wife he could afford to give a lot more to his present one, and temper threatened to choke her as she recalled how he had asked her to limit her clothes spending.

Without stopping to think she went into the sitting room and burned the statement and envelope in the open fire. When Ralph returned, she got him to run her into town and bought some staggeringly expensive curtains for the bedroom. For the bed itself she chose white draperies, as different from Julia's red brocade as she could possibly find.

And the mattress could go as well, she decided grimly. And the sheets and the blankets and pillows and bedspread, and the stool where Julia had sat before the dressing table. If Grant found himself short this month as a result, his ex-wife would just have to wait a while for her money. She booked the alarming total to his account without a qualm, the store promised to have it all delivered the following week, and she defiantly took a taxi for the ten-mile journey home.

It didn't last of course. Nervous reaction had settled in by the time he returned two days later and she found herself studying his face, trying to judge if there was any difference in his manner. The existence of her overdraft might be paltry in comparison with her own discovery, but hers was one she had to keep to herself.

He kissed her in greeting and was apparently normal, but when they were preparing for bed and she emerged from the bathroom once more in her nightdress, he observed acidly, 'Either it's time you saw a doctor or you're telling me something.'

Unable to meet his eyes, she flushed. For over a week she had clung to the nightdress, using the unspoken signal to keep him at arm's length and postpone the moment she must eventually face.

'Which is it?' he demanded.

Feeling the colour flare higher, she said, 'Neither.' Grant's gaze became coldly assessing and she shrugged. 'It was different in the apartment where there were only the two of us. I don't feel comfortable at the thought of sleeping in just my skin with Mrs Matthews in the house.'

'That doesn't answer the real question,' he pointed out grimly.

For a second the urge to tell him the truth was almost uncontrollable. Wild, rash sentences formed in her brain. She wanted to attack him—to ask how he expected her to feel desire in this house, in this room, where the very air she breathed reminded her that she was only a substitute for another woman—to tell him it made her feel sick to sleep in the bed he had shared with his ex-wife, knowing he need only half-close his eyes until her features were blurred to him and he could imagine it was Julia still.

With a superhuman effort she forced the thoughts down. Once spoken they could never be withdrawn and there was no hope for their marriage at all if she goaded Grant into abandoning his pretence and telling her things she had no wish to hear.

Still waiting for her reply he said, 'Well?'

Defeatedly she muttered, 'I don't know,' and his face enigmatic he watched her a moment longer then carried on undressing. She could sense anger beneath his controlled façade and when he got into bed it was all she could do not to flinch away from him, yet he wooed her as if she had been a reluctant virgin, at first only holding her, then kissing her throat and ears before covering her mouth with his. As he parted her lips a small spark lit in her and she returned the kiss. He smiled and began to caress her, moving his hands over her gently in the way that had always brought a slow build up of passion.

Perhaps if it had been dark the familiar tide would have enveloped her again, but she found herself staring at the red brocade curtains above her head and closed her eyes too late against the reality of where she was. The tiny flicker died and Grant felt the change. His lips became more urgent, his touch more coaxing as he used all his expertise, every art at his command, to revive her response and arouse her.

But her brain froze all reaction in her. After a while he raised his head, searching her face, and she touched her lips to his shoulder and whispered, 'It doesn't matter.'

When he moved to enter her she found she had been wrong—it did matter. Where previously her body had welcomed him, now it resisted, and what had been so easy was difficult and uncomfortable. She could not prevent an involuntary movement of retreat and Grant swore under his breath as he realised he was hurting her. She said, 'It's all right,' but he still hesitated until she drew him down on her. If she had shown any other sign of protest she knew he would not have continued.

Afterwards she suspected he wished he hadn't. Lying in the darkness he said harshly, 'My apologies for the rather juvenile ineptitude. The truth is that I've never made love before to a woman who was merely obliging me. We all live and learn.'

We do indeed, Fran thought wearily. It was apparent that it would be of no use to pretend a desire she didn't feel in order to salvage Grant's sexual pride. Purely physical evidence over which she had no control would always give her the lie.

CHAPTER EIGHT

GRANT was curt with her at breakfast. They hardly spoke, and he finished eating and was gone while she still toyed listlessly with a single slice of toast. He had started to break in a couple of his young horses and would probably be gone till lunch time. Fran sat at the piano and doggedly practised her scales and exercises, though her mind kept returning to the previous night and her concentration was poor. In one bar she made the same mistake over and over again. Annoyed with herself she determined to get it right, vaguely hoping at the same time that she was irritating Mrs Matthews.

It was perhaps the twentieth time she had played it when Grant burst in. His face white with rage he exploded, 'For God's sake, give it a rest! How the hell do you expect me to get any writing done with that racket in the next room!'

He was breathing quickly, his hands clenched at his sides, and for a moment she was frozen over the keys. He had pushed the door open so violently that it slammed into the sideboard, rocking all the ornaments dangerously. Wetting her lips, she said in quick nervousness, 'I'm sorry, I thought you were out. You usually write in the afternoon and evening.'

'Try looking through the window,' he invited with biting sarcasm. 'Nobody in their right mind would go out in rain like that unless they were forced to.'

'I'm sorry,' she repeated. 'I know it's raining, but you could have been out in the car somewhere. You don't tell me what you're doing half the time.'

'And you don't ask,' he retorted harshly. He paused

148

in an attempt to bring his temper under control. 'Fran, you do nothing but moon round this house all day looking discontented. All right, I've noticed and you've made your point. We'll go back to London in the autumn—six months here for me, six months there for you. Now do you think you could possibly make my half a little easier? There must surely be *something* you can interest yourself in apart from that bloody piano!'

Ostentatiously Fran closed the lid and twisted round on the stool to face him. Inside she was quivering, her own temper as high as his. 'Embroidering cushion covers?' she suggested sweetly. 'Visiting old Mrs Burgess in the village?'

His mouth tightened ominously but for once she didn't care. It had been intended as a jibe at Julia and she had intended him to know it.

He swung on his heel but turned back in the doorway, his expression bleak. 'It wouldn't do you any harm,' he told her blisteringly. 'You do damn all else!'

He slammed the door and Fran sat where she was feeling ashamed. She *could* go to see Mrs Burgess—she nearly had done the last time she visited her aunt, but she had been too unsure of herself. She was Fran, the blacksmith's niece, and she had been afraid that if she tried to take over Julia's role it would prove a resounding failure.

Grant emerged from his study for lunch and once more they ate in almost total silence. As they were drinking their coffee, Fran said, 'Grant, I'm sorry about this morning.'

'Forget it.'

His tone was indifferent and she drew a deep breath. 'I'll make sure I never do it again and I've apologised. At least accept it.'

'All right.' He leaned forward and put his cup down on the table with an abrupt movement. 'I admit I was bad tempered anyway. The play isn't going very well.'

The frown had gone but he was still unsmiling. Fran knew it wasn't the play but the remembrance of last night and his failure to get her to respond to him that had caused his ill-temper. Somehow she had to overcome this void within her or there would be nothing to keep them together. It perhaps wasn't a good time to do it, but she had to broach the subject of Mrs Matthews as well.

Moving her cup round her saucer she said hesitantly, 'And what you said to me was right—I don't do much, but it isn't from choice.' She raised her eyes. 'I know you can't sack Mrs Matthews, but couldn't you retire her? Pay her up to the time she would be leaving anyway?'

His face settled into lines of impatience. 'Fran, you're letting her obsess you—it's preventing you from thinking straight. Even if I did pay her off, we still have to have someone living in. Quite apart from the dogs, we can't go off and leave the place empty for months on end. And it would make you highly unpopular in the village if you got rid of her after all the years she's been here, not to mention making your aunt uncomfortable.'

Depressed, Fran said, 'I suppose you're right, but you don't know what it's like having her here all the time.' She caught his sardonic gaze and realised how stupid her remark must sound to him. 'I can't do anything in the house without her watching and silently criticising, and I never know when she's creeping up on me.' She took a deep breath. 'If I move things she alters them back.'

'You'll just have to assert yourself more,' he said, his impatience open now.

Fran knew he couldn't understand how difficult she found it to assert herself over someone so much older. The war over moving things had been going on for several days. To Grant it would seem trivial and petty, but Fran knew it was more than a malicious game. Mrs Matthews was determined that nothing in the house should be changed. To her, it was a shrine to the living. Perhaps it was to Grant as well. Perhaps she was just meant to fit into it exactly as it was, four inches taller and eight years younger than the woman whose place she had taken, but in all other respects the same.

Grant stayed in his study all evening, and he was still there when Fran went to bed. She lay reading, then became aware that the faint sound of the typewriter had ceased and he was coming up. Apprehension made her suddenly tense, but she realised there was no need for it when he switched his own light off at once and turned his back to her. As he settled the bedclothes round himself he said, 'Carry on reading if you want to.'

For a moment she was stunned. Always before, even when they had rowed, he had kissed her or made some sort of gesture before he went to sleep. She said, 'Grant . . .?'

He half-raised his head from the pillow in mute question, and after a moment she said numbly, 'Nothing.'

Still with his head raised he allowed a pause, then said in a level voice, 'I've paid some money into your account, by the way. You should have told me you were overdrawn—it doesn't reflect very favourably on me, particularly when it's with the same bank.'

She tried to summon back some of the angry bravado that had made her order all the new things for the bedroom, but there was only a sick dread. At the first opportunity she rang the store and tried to cancel them, but most of them were being specially made and it was too late. Thankfully, both Grant and Mrs Matthews were out when they arrived. She felt as though she really would have died if they had been there to witness the new mattress being carried in and up the stairs. She gave the delivery men a generous tip to manoeuvre the old one into the attic, and knew that they too were puzzled as to why an expensive, good-quality item in perfect condition was being stored away in the dust.

She hastily re-made the bed and hung the curtains. When she had finished she realised she had merely made the room look dull by her efforts and the flounced white curtains round the bed were totally out of keeping. During the afternoon, Grant observed cynically, 'I see you've been busy,' but he made no other comment. She supposed he must eventually have received the bill.

If the new mattress had proved to have any magic properties it would all have been worth it, but it didn't. Grant was a man with a high sex drive but he turned to her less and less. When he did it was no longer lovemaking, but a silent sating of lust. Because he knew he could no longer arouse her he ceased to make the attempt, rolling quickly away from her afterwards to leave her staring into the darkness with a tension in her body which would neither build up nor recede. Finally, his demands stopped altogether. She suspected he was afraid that one night he might find himself impotent with her and the risk of humiliation outweighed his desire.

Strangely, they now developed an easier relationship. Grant bought her a horse, which she loved, and riding round she re-discovered some of her childhood friends who had married locally. Most of them had children, and she remembered how badly she had once wanted to have Grant's child. When they first came back she had asked him tentatively if he would like a family. He had been a long time replying, and then he had said, 'If you would.' It hadn't been the answer she wanted so she had waited. She was never likely to have one now, and visiting friends who were mothers left her feeling restless and dissatisfied.

It was Grant's birthday in June and she toured countless secondhand shops for an out-of-print book which she knew he wanted. Flushed with triumph, she handed it to him, beautifully wrapped, on the day. She held her breath as he took the paper off, ridiculing herself because she was placing so much store on him liking it, and relaxed when she saw his smile of pleasure.

'It's in good condition,' she pointed out. 'All pages present and correct. I checked.'

He put it carefully down on the table, then pulled her towards him and kissed her forehead. 'You're a clever girl. I've been looking for it for years. Where did you manage to find it?'

'A bookshop near Ross, but I searched dozens before that. I did come across another one, but all the notes and Bibliography were missing from the back and it was terribly tatty besides.'

'This one's a beauty.' He picked it up to examine it again and smiled at her. 'Thank you.'

He went back to his study shortly afterwards, But Fran was light-hearted, and in the afternoon, on impulse, she went in to him and said, 'Grant let's go out somewhere tonight—just the two of us.'

He looked up in quick surprise, and she added nervously, 'Unless you're busy.'

For a moment he was silent, then he swung his chair round away from the typewriter. 'No, I'm not particularly busy. Where would you like to go?'

'Just for a meal somewhere.'

'Any preference?'

'No. At least . . .' She wavered, then went on, 'I think I'd like to go somewhere we haven't been before. Perhaps a bit further afield.'

'All right. I'll see what I can come up with.'

He reached for his diary and began to thumb through

the telephone numbers and addresses in the back, and Fran left him to it and went back to dead-heading the roses in the garden. A few minutes later he opened his study window and called, 'Booked.'

She looked up, sweeping the hair from her eyes with the back of her hand, and anticipating her question, he told her, 'It's a hotel where I've stopped for lunch a couple of times.' His eyes took in her tousled hair and the old skirt she had put on for gardening, and he smiled faintly. 'You'll need to wear something rather more sophisticated than your present attire.'

'I won't disgrace you,' she returned gaily, then bit her lip as she saw his smile fade.

Expressionless now, he said smoothly, 'That, my dear, is one thing I have never been afraid of.'

Her eyes blind with tears, Fran went on cutting the withered blooms. It hadn't been a good idea and she was tempted to tell him to forget all about it. Things were better when neither of them offered more than polite friendship. Her heart aching, she remembered how they had once laughed together. Her occasional disasters in cooking and the time she had turned all his shirts blue in the wash had seemed funny to them, but now there was never any laughter.

The hotel was an hour's drive away, and when they got there the forecourt was crowded so that Grant had difficulty in parking. Inside he surveyed the packed lounge with a frown and said, 'I'm sorry, I'm afraid you're going to have to stand. The place seems to have become a lot more popular since I was last here.'

He found her a space in the corner of the bar, then moved further along to get their drinks. Immediately he was hailed by a group from the other end, and Fran saw they were part of the wealthy crowd who owned summer cottages by the river on the scenic borders with Wales. They were a free-spending, hard-drinking set which Grant quietly despised, and her heart sank when they beckoned her over.

Hesitantly she accepted the seat they offered her and hoped Grant would extricate her once he'd got their drinks. The wives measured success by the amount of jewellery they could boast and the depth of their winter tan, and she knew they were wondering why a well-known personality like Grant should have married an obscure model.

It was Grant they were interested in, not her. Subtly patronising, one of the women asked her what it was like being married to someone famous, and in self-defence Fran began stressing the false glamour of the parties and dinners.

She was talking animatedly, making it sound exciting and enviable, when she became aware of Grant's silent presence at her shoulder. How long he had been listening she didn't know, and she flinched inwardly as his sardonic gaze flickered over her. He handed her drink to her and moved away, and she watched him playing up to the muted adulation he was receiving, acting out the part of the celebrity and secretly demonstrating to her his contempt of the flattery. Meeting his eyes she saw the glitter of mockery there, as much for her as the others she knew, and thought grimly that she didn't need a morality play from him to point out the shortcomings of the present company.

She made no objection when it was suggested they should all eat together, though Grant agreed without consulting her anyway. They were seated opposite each other and she could see him deliberately exerting all his charm on the women on either side of him. He was arrestingly handsome and his looks alone were enough to turn any woman's head, though until tonight he had never given any sign that he was aware of his own attraction. He was behaving abominably, but she was the only one who knew it because the two women were too dazzled to realise he was laughing at them.

Seething, she turned to the man on her right. He had made overtures earlier but her cool response discouraged him and she knew he had dismissed her as good looking but dull. Now, she gave him a slow smile and switched on the sex appeal she had been taught to project for the camera.

She saw the man pause in eating and look quickly across at Grant, and said smoothly, 'Isn't that your wife?'

Her message was plain. Grant's conduct with his wife meant they were in no position to complain. She let her eyes convey an invitation, and the man—searching her memory she recalled his name was Ralph—leaned towards her. From the other side of the table she saw Grant's gaze flick towards her and realised he had never seen her like this before, deliberately enticing. She smiled at him, the same inviting smile she had given Ralph, challenging him to object to what she was doing, and after a moment he gave her a glance of amused contempt and turned back to Ralph's wife at his side.

She wasn't sure whether it was the amusement or the derision which stung most, but after that she behaved outrageously. By the end of the evening there wasn't one of the wives who didn't hate her and Ralph was under the impression that she was eager to join him for a week-end on his yacht if she could escape her husband. By now Grant was far from amused by her, but she thought defiantly that it served them all right. It would teach them to be more careful whom they patronised in the future.

It was late by the time the gathering finally broke up, and she and Grant were the last to leave. When they got to the forecourt the Daimler was standing alone, and she heard Grant mutter an obscenity under his breath.

He strode quickly towards it, and following at a slower pace, Fran asked, 'What is it?'

Curtly, he said, 'Someone's slashed the tyres.'

She saw then that the angle of the car was down at the back and there were deep, zigzag scratches scored in the paintwork.

'Who could do such a thing?' she said, sick with disgust.

'Perhaps the wife of one of the men who was making a play for you,' he suggested with grim humour. He shoved at one of the tryes with his foot. 'Well, I've only got one spare wheel so we're not going anywhere in it tonight. We either phone for a taxi or see if the hotel can put us up. Which would you rather do?'

'Whichever you think would be the easiest.'

He shrugged. 'If they've got a room it would be simpler to stay. I can get some new tyres put on in the morning and drive it home instead of coming back for it.'

The hotel had got a room and the night porter even managed to provide them with a toothbrush. Otherwise of course, they had nothing. Coming out of the bathroom, Fran debated whether to sleep in her bra and pants, but she could imagine Grant's mocking reaction if she did, so she undressed hurriedly and pulled the clothes up round herself while he was washing. He suffered from no such constraints himself and moved unselfconsciously round the room, hanging up his shirt and laying his clothes flat since he must wear them tomorrow.

Slow, insidious warmth began to steal through her as she followed him with her eyes. The strange room, the unaccustomed quantity of wine she had drunk, Grant's powerful nakedness, all combined to set her pulses throbbing. She caught his eye and swallowed, and for a second his movements were arrested before he carried on folding his trousers into their creases.

The bed was narrower than their king-size one at

home and his hip brushed against her as he was tossing
one of his pillows on to the floor. The contact told him
she was equally naked and she waited tensely to see if
he would react. She dared make no move herself. Her
behaviour earlier had angered him and he was quite
likely to reject her. Any advance must come from him.

It seemed a long time that she waited, but then he
turned towards her. Holding her with his eyes he
reached out slowly and ran his hand down her throat,
then onward to enclose her breast. She quivered, and a
deep shudder of delight shook her. As though unable to
believe the evidence of touch he drew back the sheet to
expose her tautly erect nipples to his gaze, and
satisfaction leapt in his eyes as he lowered his head to
draw first one then the other into his mouth.

Desire flamed in her, catching her breath with its
violence, her need all the more desperate for having lain
so long dormant. Grant gave a husky laugh as he
transferred his lips to hers, and exultantly she felt the
manifestation of his arousal hard against her thigh.

His hand left her breast and slid downward but she
pushed it away. She wanted only to feel his weight and
the strength of his passion, and she twisted her body
round, fitting it to his.

He moved until he was poised over her, and
whispered, 'Now? Do you want me now?'

She nodded, clutching his shoulders, her fingers
biting into his flesh, but still he didn't move. Half on a
sob, she said, 'Please, Grant ... oh, please ...' and
suddenly, shockingly, he lifted himself away from her.

Stunned, she stared at him, unable to believe at first
that he wasn't merely tantalising her. Then she saw the
remorseless set of his features, and he said savagely,
'And now *you* know what it feels like!'

He sat up, pulling his pillow up behind him. Though
she knew his desire had been as high as her own he gave

no sign of it. Regarding her with narrowed eyes he was utterly unmoved as the hectic flush faded from her skin, leaving it white.

His voice harsh he told her, 'I've been waiting all evening for that little volte-face of yours—I could see it coming. You positively sparkled down there in the dining room, leading all those poor fools on and turning yourself on at the same time. But someone should have warned you, darling, that no man likes being used as a surrogate. I may not have a yacht and a villa in the Bahamas like Ralph, but I do have enough pride left not to warm myself at the fire he lit!'

Mutely she turned her head away, hardly crediting what she was hearing, and he went on mercilessly, 'It's too late, my lovely wife—I've learned to do without you. I'm not likely to risk reviving all that frustration again because you've had a delightful evening and you're prepared to dispense a few favours for once. If you ever decide it's me you want, just me, without the aphrodisiac of parties and other men's admiration, then let me know and we'll talk about it, but for now, no thanks. It's not worth it.'

Contemptuously he turned his back on her, leaving her filled with bitter hurt and rage. Hurt because he could believe what was so completely untrue, and rage because he dared to talk to her of surrogates when that was all she was to him herself.

She would have left him next morning, but when they got home, only two dogs rushed out to greet them. Ruff was dying.

Jon, their neighbouring vet, was already with her, and he shook his head at Grant's frowning look of enquiry. 'I'm sorry,' he said. 'I'm afraid it's just old age and there isn't a cure for it. Shall I . . .?'

Grant nodded, his lips tightening, and Fran turned quickly and went out of the room. She *would* leave—for her own sake she had to, but not today while he was grieving for Ruff.

Tears flooded her eyes and she ran up to the bedroom. When she saw Grant again at lunch time they were still reddened with crying, and he said quietly, 'She was an old dog and she was almost blind. It had to happen.'

Choked, Fran put her knife and fork down with a clatter, fumbling for her handkerchief to stem the silent flow of tears. He came round the table and held her, pressing her down-bent head against his shoulder, and she knew he must still feel something for her—enough to make him want to comfort her and ease the ache of loss, even when his own sorrow must be so much greater.

For a few weeks she let herself drift. One day something else would happen which would tip the balance and she would take the final irrevocable step. This was the time for preparing her mind, making herself accept the inevitable, and it was curiously peaceful.

She no longer cared what Mrs Matthews thought of her, she and Grant treated each other with calm good manners, and the weather was glorious. She spent most of each afternoon up on the hill, idly picking the wild strawberries within her reach and watching the activity of the campers down by the river. Sometimes the dogs tracked her to her hideout, and once Grant was with them. He let himself down beside her, remarking, 'So this is where you get to.'

She nodded, wondering if he would realise it was the same spot where that fatal mistake of hers had driven him away. Remembering, she felt a faint stirring of the old excitement, and somehow it seemed to communicate itself to him, like waves picked up from the air. Without being told, she knew he was remembering as well.

She looked across at him, seeing the once-familiar

sensuality in his expression, and suddenly he was kissing her and the wild response was back. As his mouth probed hers, her hands ran under his shirt, pulling him on to her with instant, fierce desire.

He groaned triumphantly, snatching at the buckle of his belt, then let out a vicious obscenity, and over the pounding of the blood in her ears, Fran heard the voices of a group of hikers calling to each other in the nearby woods.

He sat up, swearing steadily, then rose and pulled her to her feet.

'Come back to the house!'

She followed him willingly, the heat still coursing through her as she stumbled and slid down the path, carried onward by a rush of desire which lasted until he pushed her into the bedroom and began to strip her clothes away from her with frenzied, trembling haste.

Then the coldness settled back, paralysing her. Grant's voice, low and harsh with emotion washed round her, and despair filled her because it was no longer in her to give him what he wanted. But he hadn't sensed it yet, she realised, and she put her arms deliberately round him, moving against him as she used to, whispering the words which had once broken from her without conscious thought. He made love to her violently, his passion increased by the long denial. When she knew he was nearing the moment of release she arched herself against him, uttering smothered cries, feeling satisfaction of a kind when the tension in him broke to dissolve into uncontrollable shudders.

Afterwards he drew away from her immediately, flinging himself on to his back to recover his breath, and she tried to conquer her hurt at the abrupt rejection. She wanted to reach out and touch him but his attitude warned her not to, and after a while he said bitterly, 'Don't ever bother to do that again!'

'Do what?'

'Oh, for God's sake!' he exclaimed with savage impatience. 'Did you honestly believe I wouldn't know?' He raised himself on his elbow to look at her, his expression icy. 'I've held you in my arms too many times when you weren't faking it to be fooled by you now!' He let himself fall back, one hand thrust behind his head, and in a suddenly remote voice, said, 'I could even tell the difference when you were tired sometimes and it wasn't as strong. They seem distant days now.'

She was silent for a long time. Finally, she whispered pleadingly, 'Grant, take me back to London—we were happy there. It's here—this house—that is doing it to me. I can't explain, but it is.'

'And once you're back among the bright lights you'll demonstrate how grateful you are,' he returned viciously. 'Oh no, madam wife! This is my home, the place where I was born, and—which is a point to be considered—the place where I work best. And I should perhaps remind you that I work from necessity as well as personal fulfilment. Money doesn't come out of a bottomless pit, and I need to be paid if I'm to go on providing you with the little luxuries which you seem to consider essential.'

His glance flicked contemptuously over the white draperies above his head, and he left a long pause before he spoke again. 'So if you want to go back you go alone.'

'Are you telling me to go, Grant?' she asked quietly.

'No, merely defining your options. Just as you did mine.' He pushed himself up and sat on the edge of the bed, turning to look at her. 'If we stay here I'm permitted to make love to a woman who lies underneath me and endures it with admirable fortitude, or we can go back to town, and in return for a life of endless artificial entertainment I can be rewarded with instant, miraculous response and the return of the girl I though I was marrying.' He shook his head. 'No, my darling, no! There's a third option open to me which you don't seem to have considered, and few would blame me if I took it!'

She had thought of it frequently, and even wondered if he had found someone else. There was obviously a danger that such an intensely physical man would seek solace elsewhere.

But jealousy pierced through her as he made the threat, and with a blind desire to wound in return, she asked, 'Did you before? Is that why Julia left you?'

'No,' he said, his voice flat. 'I was never unfaithful.'

Oh, he wouldn't be, she thought bitterly. Not to that paragon—a woman who had left him but had still been so perfect that not the smallest suggestion of criticism could be allowed. He even apparently forgave her for deserting him. Greater love hath no man.

She turned her face into the pillow, partially muffling the taunting note in her voice as she said, 'But Julia would never give you cause, would she? She wasn't extravagant and discontented and frigid!'

'No,' he returned, the very evenness of his reply warning her of the fury he was keeping under control. 'And keep your jeering, spiteful little tongue off her!— in terms of sheer worth she'd make twenty of you!'

She rolled on to her side and watched him pick his clothes up from the floor, his face contorted with anger. Because he could never say anything worse to her— nothing that could possibly hurt more than those last words—she asked, 'Why did she leave you?'

He sent her a bitter glance, pausing in buttoning up his shirt, and his voice flat with contempt, said, 'I wouldn't give you the satisfaction of hearing me say it.'

What satisfaction could it give her? she wondered, watching again as he slid his shoes on, snatching his finger out of the back of each one with a jerky movement which told of the suppressed rage still boiling under the surface. He stood up and swung round to face her again.

'But one thing I will tell you! If she suddenly appeared before me now, my God, there are a few things we could get straightened out between us!'

CHAPTER NINE

THERE could be no more waiting in the hope that a miracle might happen and that first idyllic happiness be restored. Fran rang to find if her bed was still spare and was grateful when Sacha only said, 'Is it the, "I'll teach him to be such a swine", kind of thing, or is it for keeps?'

'It's final,' Fran said, her voice quivering.

Swiftly, Sacha said, 'Don't bother with explanations now, sweetie, they'll do when you arrive. When is it likely to be?'

Fran couldn't tell her because she didn't really know herself. She planned to leave some time during the following week while Mrs Matthews was away and she could make her preparations without arousing suspicion, but otherwise she would just make her escape when the opportunity presented itself. At the back of her mind she was convinced that in spite of everything Grant would prevent her going if he could.

There wasn't really a great deal that she had to do. Clothes she didn't want she took into the village for the next charity sale, and only the insurance papers and the bill of sale for her car proved difficult. Grant kept them in his desk in a drawer which was usually locked but she eventually managed to extract them. She waited then for a day when she could be certain he would be out long enough for her to pack and be well clear of the district before he discovered her absence.

Perversely, for several days he hardly left the house, but when she was beginning to despair he announced one morning that he would be going to Worcester the following day and wouldn't be back until evening.

She dare not speak to him before he left in case she betrayed herself and she watched him go from the window, wondering if she would ever see him again. When the car was lost from sight behind the hedges she ran up to the bedroom and followed its progress over the river and through the valley until it was only a tiny, moving blue shape. When it finally disappeared she still stared at the spot where she had last seen it, racked by sobs and an unbearable grief for the happiness she had once known and had lost.

The crying jag left her throat raw and her head throbbing. She made herself a cup of coffee in the silent kitchen and took some painkillers, knowing she must pull herself together and control her thoughts or she would be unfit for the drive.

But her thoughts wouldn't be controlled. She had to leave Grant a letter, but when she tried to compose it she found she was crying helplessly again and she couldn't see the page. The only word she could think of was goodbye, but she couldn't write it and in the end she crumpled the paper into a tiny unreadable ball and threw it in the waste bin. When she got to Sacha's and her astringent company had worked its balm she would have a stiff drink, two stiff drinks, and ring him.

She splashed cold water on her eyes and stood by the window for a moment breathing deeply, then pulled two suitcases down from inside the wardrobe and began to assemble her things on the bed. To break the silence of the empty house she switched on her small radio, but the DJ's cheerful voice and songs of lost love both grated equally on her nerves and she turned it off again. Better the silence. Then she thought she heard the sound of someone on the landing and whirled quickly.

Grant was standing in the doorway watching her, his face empty of all expression. His eyes left her to slowly scan the room, resting briefly on the pulled-out drawers and open wardrobe, and finally on her half-packed case and the pile of clothes on the bed.

Shock at his appearance held her still. She went to speak, but at first her throat seemed paralysed. She swallowed, then said, stupidly and unnecessarily, 'I'm leaving, Grant.'

'So I gathered,' he said, without inflexion. He advanced further into the room and thrust his hands into his pockets, reviewing her preparations with an apparent calm which she found more unnerving than rage. 'I've known you were planning it for some time.'

'How . . .?' she began, then fell silent, biting her lip.

'How did I know?' His smile was grim, only half-hiding his temper now. 'You forget this isn't new to me. It's all happened before and I can recognise the signs.'

He walked across the room and pulled open the drawer of her dressing table. Taking out the large brown envelope he spilled the contents out on the table top. 'Passport, medical card, driving licence, insurance, letters—you've had them collected together for a week now.' He glanced at her, and crossing to the wardrobe, pulled the doors open to their full width. 'And you must think me very unobservant if you hoped I wouldn't notice that half your clothes were missing.'

Tonelessly, Fran said, 'I thought I'd save you the trouble of clearing out after me.'

'How considerate of you.' He paused, his hand still on the door, then said with menacing emphasis. 'But rather too hasty, because now you can put all those things back!'

Meeting the unrelenting coldness in his expression she felt her nerves jump and was tempted to obey him. There would be other opportunities and the thought of continuing this confrontation made her feel sick. But he would be watching her in future. Having got this far it would be better to get it over with.

Lifting her head, she said defiantly, 'No.'

'Why argue? I took the keys out of your car as I came in so you're not going anywhere.'

He saw her defiance fade, her shoulders slackening in acknowledgement of defeat. His eyes narrowing in an unpleasant smile, he said, 'Tell me, my dear wife, since I presume this exodus was the prelude to eventual divorce, what did you propose to tell the judge was the cause of the irretrievable breakdown of our marriage? What evidence do you think you can call up to prove that my behaviour was so unreasonable that you found it impossible to go on living with me?'

She was silent, and his voice hardening, he demanded, 'Well? Do I get drunk? beat you? fail to maintain you in the style you expected?' A sardonic note entering, he said, 'Nor can you accuse me of adultery, in spite of an obvious temptation to go out and seek what I find so lacking in my own bed.' He shook his head. 'Under the circumstances, I think the court would be more likely to contratulate me on my forbearance.'

She said jerkily, 'There are other, more subtle means of making yourself intolerable, which I'm sure they must realise, but I wasn't thinking of those sort of grounds anyway. It's only necessary to have lived apart for two years.'

'Ah, but that only applies in undefended petitions with the respondent's consent,' he reminded her softly. 'And I should defend.'

Her eyes flew to his face. Chilled by the remorseless set of his features, she whispered, 'But why? What good would it do you?'

'Let's just say I have no desire to have everyone assume me to be the villain of the piece a second time.'

With sudden bitterness, she said, 'It must be wonderful to be so completely convinced of your own blamelessness. The rest of us are usually a little more honest.' Drawing a deep breath to steady herself she went on, 'But I'm still leaving, with or without my things. You can't lock me up so there's no way you can stop me.'

'Not physically,' he agreed. 'But before you do anything irrevocable I suggest we have a frank discussion. Shall we sit down?'

Fran hesitated, then sank on to a nearby chair and watched as he pushed her clothes aside to sit on the bed.

Evenly, he said, 'In the first place, let me make it clear you will wait the full five years for a divorce. If you put in a petition before then I shall defend it and believe me, you'd lose.'

He paused, observing her dismay, though she knew he had misjudged the cause. She wasn't really concerned about when their marriage officially ended. It was the thought that it would be done in a spirit of hostility and rancour that appalled her.

She lowered her lashes, trying to appear unaffected, and he continued, 'Secondly, don't fondly imagine I shall keep you during all this time. Once you walk out of here, that's it. You can sue for maintenance but I wouldn't advise it. By the time my lawyers had finished with you and it had been plastered all over the more sensational papers, you'd have achieved nothing beyond a very damaging notoriety. Think about it.'

'I don't need to!' she flashed scornfully. 'I'm not asking for anything from you.' She felt a sterile satisfaction at the fleeting surprise in his eyes. Almost immediately it was replaced by cynicism, and fighting to keep a note of pleading from her voice, she asked, 'Why can't we be civilised about this, Grant? What's the point in opposing me and making me wait for a divorce? You'll be tying yourself as well as me.'

'True, but it won't affect me.' He saw the unspoken question in the quick glance she sent him and his lips twisted. 'I don't subscribe to the theory of third time lucky. I don't think I've got the stomach for another attempt.'

He stood up and turned away from her, and she frowned, at a loss to know why he wanted this empty marriage to continue. Eventually, she said, 'In effect, you are saying you want me to stay.'

'That's the substance of it, yes.'

'Why?'

'Perhaps I want what you promised me and put your name to in the presence of witnesses.'

'*You* didn't feel bound by the promises you made before,' she pointed out acidly. 'Why should I be bound by them now?'

He swung back swiftly, his face tight with rage, and she found she was pressing herself back against the chair. The leaping anger gradually died, and he said silkily, 'Perhaps I want a reasonable return on my outlay—or just my pound of flesh.'

'Or perhaps you merely want to keep me here to avoid another admission of failure!'

'Why not? No man likes exposing himself to ridicule and our separation wouldn't be just a local affair. I don't feel like advertising to the world at large that I was fool enough to be infatuated by a lovely face.'

'You astonish me,' Fran retorted bitterly. 'I thought it was my body. You told me once that desire wasn't everything, but in your case it seems that it was. Once it was dead there was nothing left!'

With a return of the swift anger, he said harshly, 'Remember it was you who killed it!' He stared down at her, his expression brooding. 'And you knew how to do it, didn't you, my lovely wife? How to give a hint of hope then smash it! Sometimes you would respond when I kissed you and I'd think that this time it was going to be different—that we were going to get back what we had in the beginning, then suddenly—nothing. You'd switched off and I was trying to make love to a lifeless body. No reaction, no response, no feeling—nothing. You never actually refused me because you knew you didn't need to. What you were doing was mental castration—a little slower, perhaps, but in the end it works as well as any knife!'

'It wasn't deliberate, Grant,' she protested despairingly. 'It wasn't anything I could help.' She checked, wondering why it should still seem important even now to try to convince him, then shrugged helplessly as she met his open disbelief. 'I would have thought that by thirty-eight you'd have learned that some women need more than mere expertise to rouse them. They're affected by surroundings and atmosphere and all sorts of other things that men don't consider important.'

'If I didn't know before you'd certainly have taught me!' he returned savagely. 'Oh, you can be turned on by atmosphere all right! Give you parties and theatres and more expensive clothes than you can wear and you're instantly every man's dream!'

'That isn't true!' she flared. Clenching her hands, she heard the quiver of impotent fury in her own voice. 'I'm not going to bother to deny it again because nothing I say will ever alter what you choose to think. Carry on being blameless if it makes you feel better, but believe it or not there are some women who need to feel they are more than just an object of desire. It works for a while, but on its own it isn't enough. They need the other kind of love as well.'

'So?'

She looked up to find him studying her impatiently. 'You've lost me somewhere. How does all this apply to us? You're surely not trying to make out I only married you for your body?' When she was silent he added with deliberate brutality, 'If you remember, you offered it to me without!'

A tide of colour rose up her face, but she kept her voice level. 'No, that was only part of it. I'm saying that you married me not for what I am but for what you thought I was.'

'At least we're agreed on one thing! But if that little speech a moment ago was meant to tell me something, I'm afraid I don't get it. Just what did you want or expect that I failed to give you? What *do* you want, Fran?'

'Nothing,' she said dully. 'Or nothing you can give me anyway.'

She wrenched her gaze away to stare at the clothes and cases on the bed, blinking to disperse a rush of tears. With a sudden desire to inflict some of her own pain on Grant, she said viciously, 'Go back to your precious Julia and beg her to forgive you! God knows you're paying her enough to keep her sweet!'

She got up to walk away but his hand shot out and grabbed her wrist, dragging her back. Icily, he demanded, 'And how would you know that?'

She tried to twist free but his grip on her only tightened, his fingers biting in until the flesh underneath went numb. In quick fear, she said, 'The postman got our statements crossed. I opened yours without realising and I saw the standing order.' The fear faded and she met his eyes, her own hard. 'Don't you think it's perhaps unwise to give her so much? She's not likely to marry again if it means losing a steady income for life.'

Softly and contemptuously, he said, 'You little bitch.'

'I was only being practical. The way things are you could hardly afford much in the way of maintenance so it would be pointless to ask for it.'

She snatched her wrist free and thought for a second that he was going to strike her. He was pale round the mouth with anger, but then with a visible effort he controlled himself. In a flat voice, he said, 'I suppose it was stupid of me not to guess when I opened your statement that you must have had mine. It answers a lot of questions.'

Despairingly, Fran wished she had held her tongue. Grant said with savage scorn, 'So that's what has been eating away at your avaricious little soul. I wasn't quite the meal ticket you thought, so you want to go out in search of a better one.'

She didn't reply and his eyes swept over her derisively. Reaching into his pocket he drew out her car keys and tossed them to her as though her touch might contaminate him. 'Then I won't stand in your way, darling—you can have your divorce. And you can keep the car.'

Through stiff lips, she retorted, 'How magnanimous of you. Since it's registered in my name there isn't a great deal you could do about it, but thank you, I will keep it. In spite of your rather nauseating self-righteousness it wasn't all as one-sided as it suits you to believe, and I think I deserve that much out of the wreck.'

'What's that supposed to mean?'

Sick and unutterably weary, she said, 'Oh, why bother to pretend at this stage? We both know you only married me because I reminded you of Julia.'

For the space of a few seconds he seemed stunned. He stared at her, his expression blank with disbelief, then, his voice rising, he demanded, 'Are you insane?'

Shocked by his tone, suddenly uncertain, she said, 'Why should I be insane? What do you mean?' and with an incredulous glitter in his eyes he began to laugh, harshly, but with genuine amusement. 'Is that what you believed? Christ Almighty, do you mean you *didn't* know?'

His violent words seemed to ring round the room, confusing her. Bewildered, she repeated, 'What do you mean? What should I have known?'

His laughter mocking now, he told her with ironic bitterness, 'I only married Julia because she reminded me of *you*!'

For a moment the world seemed to spin backwards, half-formed thoughts whirling in her brain, then settling into a meaningless disorder of which she could make no sense. She whispered finally, 'I don't understand. Why . . .?'

His voice searing, he broke in, 'Because I had to do *something*! You were *fourteen*, for God's sake, and you were driving me out of my mind! I was obsessed with you!—a man of twenty-eight! Can you imagine what the men in the village would have done if they'd known the thoughts I was harbouring about you? If I'd acted them out I wouldn't even have been safe in prison!'

He flung away from her and went to stand by the window. His tone flat with self-contempt, he said, 'I despised myself, but there was nothing I could do about it. I kept telling myself how old you were—repeating it like a litany whenever I was near you—but I couldn't *think* of you as a child—you didn't look like one or seem like one.'

He paused for a moment, then went on, 'I almost convinced myself that as long as I never touched you or let you see what I felt, then it was all right, I wasn't doing any harm, but I knew I was wrong. I should have slapped you down, told you to go and practise your lures on one of the village lads instead—I realised you were sexually aware of me and it was dangerous—but I couldn't make myself. I kept thinking, I'll do it tomorrow—I'll just see her one more time, then tomorrow I'll do it.'

Turning his head, he stared sightlessly over the valley. 'I used to stand by this window to watch for you coming over the bridge. It was playing with dynamite and I knew I was a fool. One or two people had already dropped hints that I might find myself in trouble if I wasn't careful, but I managed to laugh it off and say you were just a kid. I thought I was still able to keep the situation in control. Then up on the hill that day I frightened myself sick because I so nearly wasn't in control, and I knew I had to get away from you.'

He was still staring through the window, and Fran watched him with a wild, leaping joy beginning to sing in her veins. Carefully masking all traces of emotion, she asked, 'Where did you meet Julia?'

'In London soon after I got there. I could hardly believe it at first, she was so like you it was uncanny. She'd even got some of your mannerisms—the trick you've got of turning your eyes as you look up. She seemed like you all over again, but she wasn't forbidden to me. She was a woman and I was allowed to touch her, allowed to love her.'

He leaned his head back and closed his eyes, exhaling on a long sigh. 'God, you've no idea of the relief there was in that. I felt normal again—I didn't have to bottle everything inside me or feel ashamed. I thought she was the answer to all those prayers I'd sent up—a reward for not giving in to temptation. I married her as soon as I could.'

Holding her breath, praying he wouldn't close up, Fran asked quietly, 'Why did it go wrong?'

He swung round with an abrupt movement and regarded her narrowly, then said with weary indifference, 'Oh, what does it matter now?' Half-turning away, he leaned his shoulder against the wall in the embrasure, and said at last, 'She knew about you. Don't ask me how—I can't tell you. Perhaps I talk in my sleep or perhaps it's something a woman can sense. In the beginning I thought I did love her, but I was always looking for something that wasn't there. I tried to hide it from her and we both pretended there was nothing wrong. We stayed in London for more than a year because I was afraid to bring her home, but she wanted to come back so eventually we did. We'd been here about a week when she came back from the village one day and I knew she'd seen you. She didn't tell me and I didn't ask—I don't think either of us ever mentioned your name until that night I saw you in the theatre.'

There was a long silence, and his voice raw, he said, 'She told me then that she couldn't go on with the marriage. She loved me and it was crucifying her. I persuaded her to carry on for a while and see if we could work anything out, but it was no use—you were always there between us, however much I tried to conceal it. In a way I did love her, but she knew it was only a fraction of what I felt for you.' He drew in a deep, harsh breath. 'The day she left she told me that every time I made love to her she knew I was imagining it was you I was holding in my arms. There wasn't anything I could say,' he finished bleakly. 'God help me, it was true.'

Fran made a small, involuntary movement, and his eyes slid over her without interest. In level tones, devoid of all expression, he said, 'She wrote to me and said she hoped I'd find you again. I don't think anyone has ever felt such a swine in the history of the world as I did when I read that. She'll be on my conscience until I die, and it was all for what? An illusion. Something I'd built up in my mind—an image I'd created for myself from the bright, charming little girl I'd watched growing up. I thought the woman would be the adult of the child I had known. Self-delusion doesn't take into account the fact that people change.'

Feeling the tears gather behind her eyes, Fran said huskily, 'Not always, Grant.'

He turned his head slowly towards her, and she hesitated, gathering her courage in case he repulsed her. 'Grant, why do you think I threw myself at you all those years ago?'

'Experimentation, I suppose,' he said indifferently. 'It's the usual reason at that age. You were too young to really know what you were doing, or how you affected me.'

Distinctly, she said, 'But I did know.'

He looked across at her with a quick frown, and the tears she could no longer hold back spilled over and ran down her cheeks. She met his suddenly alert stare with a slow, glimmering smile. 'You were right to go away, but oh God, Grant, you should have waited for me— you should have waited for me!'

Her voice broke on the last words and she cried openly now, but he made no move towards her. Eyes narrowed, he was tensed into an unnatural stillness.

'What are you saying?'

'That I love you, of course. I always have done, for as long as I can remember. There's never been anyone but you—I've never wanted anyone but you.'

'Then what the hell have these last months been all about?' he demanded roughly.

'It doesn't matter now.' Sobbing helplessly she reached out to him. 'Hold me, Grant—put your arms round me and hold me.'

She felt them enclose her and clung to him, her fingers pressing convulsively into his back. For a long while neither of them moved, then he began to smooth his hand up and down her shoulder in a gesture of comfort and she lifted her head and gave a choked laugh.

'I'm soaking your shirt.'

'And I suppose you've only got those useless little paper tissues.' Twisting, he reached into his pocket and proffered his handkerchief. 'Here.'

She took it from him with a muttered word of thanks and he watched while she dried her face and eyes, then said steadily, 'Now what *was* it all about, Fran?'

She shook her head. 'For an intelligent man you're a fool. Couldn't you see the same thing was happening all over again? I thought you still loved Julia—that I was a substitute, and for me it was even worse. When we came here she was all around me. I lived with all the curtains and carpets she had chosen, sat in the chairs where she had sat, slept with you in the same bed you'd slept in with her. I couldn't get rid of her, however I tried. I bought a new mattress and those curtains for the bed, but nothing made any difference—she was *here*! Sometimes I could almost *see* her!' She took a deep breath. 'And I just—froze—inside.'

Groaning, he pulled her back into his arms and cradled her. 'Fran, Fran—couldn't you have told me? Did we have to go through all that bloody misery for the sake of a few words?'

'I daren't tell you. I was afraid even to mention her name. Your face changed and you seemed to close up and shut me out every time you talked about her. It was as though she was sacred. When there was that fuss in the papers about us being alike, it was Julia you were bothered about.'

'It was conscience. I should never have married her but I did, and I was trying to protect her from being hurt any more. I felt she had a right to expect that at least.'

Fran nodded, aware of the small, hot flare of jealousy which still burned in her, and Grant said, 'What is it?'

'Nothing really.' She pulled away from him slightly. 'Time will cure it, I expect, but I've never in my life heard one single word of criticism about her and I always feel people compare us and regard me as second best. Was she so perfect, Grant?'

There was a long pause, and he said slowly, 'If you want the truth, the answer has got to be yes.' He looked down at her, his expression wry. 'She was always good tempered, always considerate, thoughtful and kind with everyone, not just me. And it was genuine—it wasn't just a front she put on for other people, it was her nature, just as she was always naturally neat and well groomed, whether we were going out or not.'

His voice altered, becoming distant with remembered thoughts. 'And I used to long for her to lose her temper with me one day, or start an argument, or leave her clothes scattered about the bedroom floor. Even to see her with a smut on her nose would have been a blessed relief. I don't think I ever swore in front of her or had a drink too many in the whole of those six years, though she wouldn't have said anything if I had, and to knowingly and deliberately do anything that might hurt her would have been like slapping an innocent, trusting child. There's nothing quite so restraining as pure goodness—it robs you of all the weapons you would normally use. You can't pick a fight and have a slanging match because you couldn't be such a bastard. It binds you, cages you, forces you to conform when you want to break out because you're irritable or angry and you need to relieve your feelings. It's bland and smothering . . .'

He paused for a moment, staring into the distance. 'God, at times it's so bloody boring that I wanted to get up and smash something!'

He ran his hands slowly down her back and said reflectively, 'I used to sit there and think of you with your scratched arms and legs and your hair flying all over the place, but it only made things worse.'

She stirred in his arms and he laughed suddenly and looked down at her again. 'You'll never be perfect, Fran, but I don't want perfection. It's too hard to live with.'

She was silent while her brain absorbed his words and broke up the image of Julia which had been created in her mind. Finally she asked on a tentative note, 'Why didn't you have children?'

'I don't think she really wanted them. Strangely enough, she wasn't very maternal, and she wasn't close to her own parents, possibly because of the way she was brought up. She was an only child and she had the usual upper middle-class background of nanny, then boarding school. She liked everything ordered, and according to my mother, children are noisy, messy little beasts. They tend to be sick on your shoulder and develop spotty complaints at the most inconvenient moments.'

Fran said, 'Yes, but . . .' then her voice trailed away as she realised it was impossible to imagine Julia with sticky fingers entwined in that smooth, elegant chignon. Her heart suddenly lightened, and she said curiously, 'Didn't you mind?'

Grant shook his head, and after another small hesitation, she said, 'Would you ever have left her?'

'No,' he said honestly. 'She loved me and that was the most binding thing of all. She believed I felt the same way in the beginning and she let me see how much. When I realised I had made a mistake I swore I would never expose myself to anyone as she had done to me. It's humiliating enough when it merely evokes pity, and it's too powerful a weapon to risk giving in to the wrong hands.'

'Is that why you never told me you loved me?'

He brought his hands up to hold her face between his palms. 'You never told me either,' he said gently. 'I never knew why you'd married me.'

'No,' she agreed. 'I was afraid to expose myself with words as well.' Slight colour tinged her face. 'But I thought I'd shown you.'

'You're hot-blooded, Fran,' he told her bluntly. 'It might not have been only for me.'

For a second her colour deepened, then she smiled. 'It was though. You've always had the same effect on me.' Half-laughing, she added, 'You're the only man I ever plotted to seduce, anyway.'

His brows lifted in query, then he looked startled. 'God, I didn't think your intentions were as serious as that!' he exclaimed. 'I'd have run sooner if I'd realised!' The amused alarm faded from his expression and he looked down at her. 'What about now, Fran? Do I still have the same effect on you?'

She smiled again, this time with deliberate provocation. 'You'll have to find out.'

He brought his mouth slowly down to hers, questioningly at first, testing for reaction with the memory of the months where there had been none, then, as her lips parted under his, with growing urgency and hunger. She felt his body harden against her, the muscles in his back tensing rigidly as his mind moved on ahead, and to her inexpressible joy and relief a tide of response flooded through her. Her breath catching, she tightened her arms round him and he lifted his head and whispered, 'Yes, darling?'

In reply she began to undo the buttons of his shirt, her fingers trembling and inept, and stilling her hands he turned and pulled the cases from the bed. In the act of sweeping her clothes to the floor, he hesitated and searched her face. 'We can go to one of the other rooms, Fran.'

She was tempted but she shook her head. She had to win here, in this room, or the echo of Julia's presence would always remain, muted perhaps, but still not completely silenced.

Momentarily the old chill formed again, but he pulled her back into his arms. His mouth on her hair, he said, 'I love you—you and only you. Don't think of anything else.'

It was the first time he had said the words to her directly, and suddenly the magic was back, flaring within her. With a muffled exclamation she turned her face into his shoulder and his hands caressed her for a moment then moved down to seek the clip on the waistband of her skirt.

Fumbling with it, he muttered with amused impatience, 'I've never understood why they have to make women's clothes so that they fasten the wrong way,' and she laughed on a clear note and reached behind to flick it undone with her finger.

He looked at her quickly and she saw the last of the doubt and tension leave him. Bending, he kissed the side of her mouth. 'I began to think I should never hear you laugh again.'

'I thought I would never want to.'

'I'll make it up to you.' He smiled as he guided her skirt over her hips, then his eyes darkened. 'This will be like it used to be, darling.'

She nodded, and his hands roved her bared flesh, revelling in the touch, then seized the hem of her jersey top to lift it over her head. He dropped it on to the floor behind her, and she heard humour threaded into the low tones as he hooked his thumb into the side of her lace briefs and said, 'Let's get you out of these concessions to decency.'

Free from them, she lay back on the bed and watched openly as he swiftly discarded his own clothes. He stood for a moment in front of her, returning her regard, then came down beside her, laughing in his throat.

'A modest, delicate woman would avert her eyes.'

'But I'm not one,' she replied frankly.

'No.' He slid his hand slowly down over her breast to her stomach, pausing as he felt a spasm in the muscles lying just under the smooth flesh. 'You're every man's secret dream—a wanton mistress for a wife.'

Surprise invading her other emotions, she turned her head quickly. 'Am I?'

'Didn't you know?'

'How could I, unless you told me? There's been no one else.'

The taut lines of his mouth altered as his lips twisted wryly. 'How could you indeed?' His hand continued downwards, and he watched her eyes darken as the pupils dilated. His voice slightly thickened, he said, 'From a much more extensive and varied experience, I can assure you that I find you—unique.'

His gaze held hers, silently giving her the final reassurance she craved, and with a slow smile she turned towards him. He was holding himself on a tight rein she knew, but some demon prompted her to prove her power over him by making him lose control. She reached out, her touch deliberately sensual and arousing, and his breath hissed sharply between his clenched teeth.

Grabbing her wrist, he exclaimed, 'Fran, for God's sake! What are you trying to do?'

She hardly knew herself, but his suddenly narrowed stare held comprehension. He murmured, 'So . . .' then rolled her roughly on to her back, holding her by the hair to position her for his descending lips, while his other hand tormented her, enflaming, then withholding until she tore her mouth free and whispered disjointedly, 'Grant, please . . . you've had your revenge . . .'

In total surrender she pulled him on to her, curving her body to receive him in a mute display of need. Her breath came out in a gasp as he responded, then they were both lost in the fierce, mindless striving towards release. It was swift and violent, a frenzy of blind desire that had built up during the weeks they had lain apart, tortured by memories. Always in the past, even at the height of passion, Grant had retained an awareness that he could unwittingly hurt her with the force of his lovemaking, but now he was unheeding and it gave her an added, primitive pleasure. Lifted to the unbearable brink she heard her own voice, shocking in its raw desperation, crying out and pleading, until the insupportable tension gave way before a convulsive, rippling ecstasy.

For a moment she was lost, cut off from everything by the intensity of feeling, then she was brought back by the savage grip of his arms and the final, crushing pressure of his full weight before he collapsed down on to her.

They remained locked together while his breathing eased, then he raised his head to look at her. She smiled faintly, only half returned to normal awareness, her pulses still thudding, and he sighed and rested his forehead against her.

'I'm sorry—I was rough with you.'

'It's all right,' she told him softly. Reaching up, she spread her fingers in the blackness of his hair. 'And anyway, you don't need to be sorry. I don't know why, but it was what I wanted. I provoked you into it.' He eased himself away and lay on his side, sliding an arm beneath her to pull her close again, and she added, 'I love you,' and rested her cheek against his chest. 'I used to tell you when you were asleep before. And inside my head.'

'We had a slight communications problem,' he said drily.

'Yes. And all our troubles could have been cured with three words—seven letters.'

'You can't count,' he told her, laughing under his breath. 'I seem to remember telling you once before that you were practically illiterate.'

'So what's one letter,' Fran retorted. She lay in drowsy contentment until a wood pigeon clattered on to the roof above the window, calling to her attention to the afternoon sunlight pouring into the room. Lifting his arm she tried to read his watch and said, 'What time is it? I can't see.'

'Twenty-past five.' He watched the dawning horror in her expression with amusement, and pulled her down again when she tried to sit up.

'Grant, let me go! Ralph will be knocking soon to say he's leaving.'

'Let him,' he said idly. 'We just don't answer the door.'

'But he'll wonder why! Both our cars are still outside!'

'I don't give a damn. It's no business of his if I want to make love to my wife in the afternoon. As long as I go down to feed the dogs there's no reason why we shouldn't stay here till morning.'

'Yes there is. If anyone else called it would be all round the village and I'm not having them smirking every time I go into the shop.' She looked round at the disorder in the room. 'Get some clothes on while I straighten this chaos.'

Half-amused, half-serious, he returned, 'Get some on yourself before I say to hell with everyone.'

She retrieved her housecoat from the pile intended for packing and made for the bathroom. When she returned from showering Grant was dressed, and from his wet hair, must have used the other bathroom. Holding her housecoat together, she gathered up her crumpled skirt and top and threw them into a corner for the laundry, then turned back to find Grant had upended the cases on to the floor and was storing them back in the wardrobe. For a moment her stomach lurched. Another half hour and she would have been gone and on her way to London.

Almost afraid to ask, she said, 'Grant, did you know I intended leaving today, or was it just chance you came back?'

His face became sombre. 'I was reasonably sure. Your petrol tank was already three-quarters full but you had it topped up again yesterday. There was no need unless you were going on a long journey.' He closed the wardrobe doors and looked across at her. 'I told you I was going into Worcester so you would think you had the afternoon clear and I could come back and catch you. I'm not really sure what I hoped to gain by it, except that otherwise I knew I should just come home one day and find you gone.'

There was a stark note in his voice as he ended, and her eyes suddenly flooding with tears, she said, 'Oh, Grant . . .' then halted, overcome by her conflicting emotions. Helplessly, she told him, 'I'm sorry.'

His smile crooked, he asked, 'Why? Was it any more your fault than mine?'

She shook her head, wiping her eyes with the back of her hand, and he pulled her against him and bent to kiss her forehead. 'Don't cry because I haven't got a handkerchief to offer you this time. It's somewhere among this conglomeration round our feet.'

Fran laughed as he had intended her to, and began to gather up the clothes and put them on hangers. Glancing through the window she caught a glimpse of the groom in the lane and turned on Grant in mild triumph. 'There, I told you—Ralph is coming now.'

'I'll go down to him.' He paused, half-way to the door. 'And to set your mind at rest I'll put both cars out of sight in the garage and lock all the downstairs doors. If anybody does call, we're out.' She laughed, an odd mixture of excitement and embarrassment, and he added softly, 'So don't get dressed again.'

He went down, and a moment later voices floated up from beneath the window, Ralph's slow spoken rumble, and Grant's quick, decisive rejoinders. Grant was trying to hurry him, but he refused to be deterred from his one-paced recital of the day's events. She opened the window a crack and Grant's words came up clearly, impatience beginning to break through in his tone.

'I'll talk to you about it in the morning, Ralph. I'm going out this evening and I haven't got time now.'

Even Ralph could hardly ignore such an obvious dismissal, and Fran devoutly hoped he didn't hear Grant putting the cars away as he went out of the gate.

It took longer to clear all the things away than it had done to assemble them, and she was closing the final drawer with a sigh when Grant shouldered the door open. He was bearing two glasses and a bottle of champagne in an ice bucket, and her brows lifted as he carefully placed them on his bedside table.

'I thought you didn't really like champagne?'

He grinned. 'I feel in the mood for it. There's something delightfully decadent about the thought of drinking it in bed. And besides, we're celebrating.'

He eased the cork out of the bottle, holding it over the ice bucket, and when he held her glass out to her, she asked, 'What's the toast?'

He held her gaze steadily. 'The next ten, twenty, thirty, forty years?'

Through blurred eyes she saw him take her glass out of her hand again, then he held her silently, her cheek pressed against his chest. 'I can live without you,' he told her quietly. 'I did before, and the world wouldn't have ended if you'd left me today, but it wouldn't have been much of a life. There's a difference between happiness and existence.'

'I know,' she said thickly. She paused to swallow the
constriction in her throat. 'I used to try to be logical
about what I felt. I told myself that if I'd been born in a
different time and a different place I should never have
met you.' She shook her head. 'But it didn't make any
difference. I couldn't bear to go on living with you as
we were, but I didn't know how I was going to live
without you either.'

Her voice broke, and he said, 'Hush, it's all over.' His
arms tightened, then he lifted her chin so he could look
into her face. 'Drink your champagne and stop thinking
about what bloody fools we nearly were. We can both
frighten ourselves to death doing that.'

He held the glass to her lips and obediently she drank
some, and said wistfully, 'I wish Mrs Matthews didn't
have to come back. We shouldn't be celebrating up here
if she wasn't away.'

With a quick, brilliant smile, he said, 'So we'll make
the most of it.' He slid his hand inside her housecoat
and lifted the swell of her breast in his palm, gently
caressing with his thumb. 'It won't be all that long
before she retires.'

She bit her lip at the insistent movement, annoyed
because she could hear laughter in his voice. Defensively,
she said, 'It's all right for you—you don't have her
dripping disapproval over you all day.' She was struck
by a sudden thought and felt warmth steal up her face.
'Oh God, I suppose she knows everything.' At Grant's
nod of confirmation she closed her eyes despairingly.
'No wonder she's hostile.'

'There's a simple cure for her.' Meeting Fran's look of
enquiry, he said, 'Stop taking that damned pill. She'll
start to mellow the moment you tell her you're pregnant.'

For a few seconds, realisation held her still. Aware of
something hidden, Grant's hand ceased its pleasurable
movement, and he asked sharply, 'What is it?'

A curious sensation washed over her and she gave a slow smile.

'I've already stopped.'

His eyes probed her face. As her smile registered, his searching frown died and his hand travelled down to rest, fingers spread, on her flat stomach. Deep inside her she felt a quiver. The act of love was designed to create life, and the thought that it might result in conception gave her a spreading, physical pleasure which had nothing to do with desire. The instinctive feeling surged through her, so strong she knew it must show in her face, and she glanced up and saw with a small shock that Grant's expression mirrored her own.

Half-questioning, she said, 'But you didn't mind about Julia. I thought you didn't want children either.'

'I did—I always have done.' His hands smoothed down her arms then gripped hard. 'But I wanted them to be ours, Fran.'

Too choked by emotion to speak she clung to him fiercely. Even more than with words of love he had shown the depths to which he was committed to her. Reaching up she pulled his head towards her until she could find his lips, exulting in the swift response she aroused. Passion hardened his mouth on hers, the hungry searching pressure feeding the rapid rise of desire. When he raised his head again she could feel the heavy beat of his heart and pulses, but the thickly lashed eyes were narrowed in a smile, and he said softly, 'This time, my darling, it's going to be different again.'

You're invited to accept 4 books and a surprise gift Free!

Acceptance Card

Mail to: **Harlequin Reader Service**®

In the U.S.
2504 West Southern Ave.
Tempe, AZ 85282

In Canada
P.O. Box 2800, Postal Station A
5170 Yonge Street
Willowdale, Ontario M2N 6J3

YES! Please send me 4 free Harlequin Presents® novels and my
free surprise gift. Then send me 8 brand new novels every month as
they come off the presses. Bill me at the low price of $1.75 each
($1.95 in Canada)—an 11% saving off the retail price. There are no
shipping, handling or other hidden costs. There is no minimum
number of books I must purchase. I can always return a shipment
and cancel at any time. Even if I never buy another book from
Harlequin, the 4 free novels and the surprise gift are mine to
keep forever.   108 BPP-BPGE

Name   (PLEASE PRINT)

Address   Apt. No.

City   State/Prov.   Zip/Postal Code

This offer is limited to one order per household and not valid to present
subscribers. Price is subject to change.   ACP-SUB-1

EYE OF THE STORM

MAURA SEGER

A powerful portrayal of the events of World War II in the Pacific, *Eye of the Storm* is a riveting story of how love triumphs over hatred. In this, the first of a three-book chronicle, Army nurse Maggie Lawrence meets Marine Sgt. Anthony Gargano. Despite military regulations against fraternization, they resolve to face together whatever lies ahead.... Author Maura Seger, also known to her fans as Laurel Winslow, Sara Jennings, Anne MacNeil and Jenny Bates, was named 1984's Most Versatile Romance Author by *The Romantic Times*.